CANDLELIGHT DREAMS

Mistletoe Meadows
Book 9

JESSIE GUSSMAN

Acknowledgments

Cover art by Covers and Cupcakes
Editing by Heather Hayden
Narration by Jay Dyess
Author Services by CE Author Assistant

Listen to the unabridged audio for FREE performed by Jay Dyess on the Say with Jay channel on YouTube. Get early access to all of Jay's recordings and listen to Jessie's books before they're available to the general public, plus get daily Bible readings by Jay and bonus scenes by becoming a Say with Jay channel member.

Books in the Mistletoe Meadows Sweet Christmas romance series:
1. Sleigh Bell Dreams
2. Icicle Dreams
3. Sugarplum Dreams
4. Christmas Dreams
5. Holly Jolly Dreams
6. Candy Cane Dreams
7. Mistletoe Dreams

Chapter One

Pastor Mark Stevens pulled slowly into the parsonage parking lot. The black shadow of the church was outlined by the brightness of the almost full moon in the sky, and the parsonage was just a dark, lonesome shadow in front.

He tried to stop the sinking of his heart. Was he crazy?

No. He knew for sure that God wanted him to go to Mistletoe Meadows and be the pastor there, taking over for Pastor Johnson, who had been the pastor for more than forty years. That much he was absolutely certain of.

But leaving his little congregation that he'd started ten years prior, the one that felt like family to him, especially since he had no family of his own... He had been an only child, and his parents had been older.

Always, his church had felt like family, comfortable and warm, and especially this time of year, around the holidays, it felt like he truly had a place to belong.

And now, he felt like he'd uprooted everything. Add in the darkness of the night, the coldness, the shadows, and the fact that he was alone, made everything feel like... he'd made the wrong decision.

Was this how Abraham felt? He had left everything he knew to follow the Lord...but he had a wife with him.

Lord, you haven't given me a wife. At least Abraham had that much. Someone to stand beside him, someone to keep him company, to encourage him when he was down, and to remind him that his job was not to make himself happy, but to follow God wherever God led.

Of course, he would be the same for her. It would give him a purpose in addition to shepherding his congregation. And... maybe there would be children, and he would guide them, encourage them, raise them up in the nurture and admonition of the Lord.

God, you trusted Abraham to raise his children. You said you knew that he would raise them for You. I would try to do that too, with everything I have.

He'd started the ministry thinking he wanted to get married and have a really big family. The kind of family that he didn't have growing up. Not that he didn't love his parents, not that he didn't understand why. They were older; maybe he was all they could have—he wasn't sure. But he had really felt the lack of siblings, and had planned to have at least ten kids of his own. Of course, finding a woman who shared that dream was a little bit more difficult. Most women wanted to have a career and a life and didn't want to be a pastor's wife, with all of the things that normally entailed.

Lord, I know you have the perfect woman for me. Or... am I supposed to be alone?

There was always that nagging thought that maybe God really didn't have the perfect woman for him. Maybe he really wasn't supposed to have a partner in this life.

As he pulled around the side of the building to park in front of the back door, where he'd carried all of his books in on the previous trip, he shuddered again, he felt more alone than he ever had in his life before. Even more alone than he had when his parents had died within a week of each other, because at least then he'd had his little pastorate and the thirty to fifty congregants that were faithful every time the doors were open. They had felt like family. Now, they'd hired a new pastor, and he had left.

But then, as he was sitting there in his car, reevaluating all of his life decisions, and wondering if he had misunderstood what God wanted for him, he saw a little flicker in the window. He tilted his head.

It was a candle. A candle whose warmth and brightness cut through the dark, encouraging him, letting him know that when he walked in the door, it wasn't going to be cold and barren, but there was a little light to guide him.

He smiled in the darkness, because it was such a great analogy for the Christian life. A lost soul, looking for something, someone, anything that would help light their way, show them what to do, give some warmth and comfort in this dark world, and that was what a Christian was supposed to be. A little light to shine for Jesus and give encouragement in the darkness of the world.

He thought often that the darker and more sinful the world got, the brighter a Christian's light would shine. And here it was in his own life—God had provided the light.

Thank you, Lord. I needed that.

God always gave him exactly what he needed. It was a promise God made. Not to fulfill his wants, but to fill his needs.

Feeling cheered, he pulled on the car latch and opened his door. After grabbing a few packages from the back, figuring the rest of it could wait until morning, he walked up the walk that he'd trudged multiple times that day and the day before, as he moved his meager belongings—and copious amounts of books, study guides, and Bibles—into the small parsonage.

It was a Cape Cod style home, with four bedrooms on the second floor, and an open floor plan on the first, except for the room he was going to use as an office.

It was probably supposed to be the master bedroom, since there was an attached bathroom, which was really nice, but the parsonage connected to the church through that room and he wanted to have the office on the first floor so that if he needed to have members of the congregation, or anyone really, over, they didn't have to go upstairs. The upstairs would be a sanctuary for his family.

I am getting a family, right, Lord? I'll follow you wherever you go, but... please?

It was a cry of his heart. He didn't really even have words anymore. He'd been asking God since he was about thirteen, praying for his wife, whoever she was, wherever she was, and that the Lord would just guide and protect her.

And lead them together when the timing was right.

He had felt like the timing had been right ten years prior, when he had started his first church, but obviously God disagreed.

He wasn't really looking forward to going in and being by himself. He already felt lonely inside, but he'd talked to Mrs. Tucker, who had asked him to leave the door unlocked from his last trip, so she could drop off supper that the congregation had donated. Obviously, Mrs. Tucker had brought a candle and left it burning as well.

His old church was only forty-five minutes away, but it felt like forever, because they already had a new pastor, and while they loved him, and he knew they always would, they'd moved on.

He opened the door, and before he even flipped on the light, the scent of fresh-baked homemade bread drifted into his consciousness.

How did that scent always make one feel like coming home?

Had Mrs. Tucker actually baked the bread in his house?

She had mentioned something about soup and a salad, and checked about allergies. She hadn't said anything about homemade bread.

Flipping the light on, he saw the candle sitting on the island in the kitchen. Flickering, the light not as bright, obviously now that the lights were on, but somehow emitting a warmth and welcome that warmed his soul.

He thought again of the analogy of the light in the Bible, how

Jesus didn't want us to hide our light, but to put it where it could be a welcoming sight for others.

What a great reminder. One he already knew, of course, but so many times he forgot. How a Christian could shine as a light, reflecting Jesus in everything they did. Giving people who were lost and hopeless encouragement and cheer in the midst of troubled times.

Two containers with lids sat on the counter, and as he drew closer, he realized that neither one of them was fresh-baked bread.

But where was that delicious smell coming from?

That's when he looked a little closer at the candle.

A label that looked to be printed off a home printer declared "Winter's Candle Shop," and the address was Mistletoe Meadows. So obviously, the candle came from someone in town. Perhaps someone who went to the church and who donated it to be a blessing to the new pastor.

Boy, were they.

The scent was: homemade bread.

That explained it. And, wow, did they nail that scent.

The salad and soup looked delicious, and the soup was still warm, so he dug around until he found the box where he'd packed the meager silverware he had, and sat down at the kitchen table. Then, before he even prayed for his food, he stood back up, grabbed the candle, and walked it over to the table.

He set it down in the middle, so he could watch it flicker and burn as he ate.

Then, setting the gifts of food and light in front of him, he bowed his head and thanked God for the blessings in his life, the new direction, and prayed that he would have discernment to see what door God was going to open for him next.

He knew that sometimes when it felt like everything was hopeless and a person had hit bottom, that's when things really turned around.

He had been doubting himself all day. Why was he leaving a

church that had been growing for years? Sure, it felt like family, but they were seeing God work and move, and thirty to fifty congregants in the rural area where he was, was a good number.

It was far more than the five that he'd started with on his first Sunday there. That had included his parents, who had since passed away.

Still, he was almost positive that God had something really special planned for him. And, as he got warm soup in his belly, made himself eat the salad because it was good for him, and enjoyed the flickering light of the candle and that delicious homemade bread smell, he began to be encouraged that taking this new pastorate could be the very best thing that had ever happened to him.

God had a way of working things like that.

Chapter Two

Olivia pushed her hair back away from her face and stretched her back to try to ease the ache in it. She had another hour of work to do before she could head home for the night.

Thankfully, the twins were still small enough to snuggle on the cot in the back room, and they'd fallen asleep hours ago.

She sighed, looking over the inventory in her candle shop as she packed another gift set, making sure to put plenty of stuffing in the box so the candle would arrive intact.

If it broke, it was on her to replace it, and it came directly out of her profits.

Plus, she didn't want people to order candles from her and have broken pieces arrive in the mail.

The mail orders had seen an uptick in the last few years, but her bread and butter were still the local orders, like the church who ordered candles for their candlelight service every year.

They always requested special candles, custom-made for that service, and then the candles that were left were burned all through the month of January, so people could bask in the glow of Christmas, even though all the other decorations were taken down.

It was a tradition Pastor Johnson had started a few years prior, and the townspeople had loved it. Several times for the Sunday evening service, they had the entire service by candlelight. It was beautiful and warm and cozy and made the winter seem not so long and dreary.

Olivia had never liked the winter, even though Winters was her last name.

Cam had joked that Winterses couldn't live somewhere where they didn't actually have a winter.

She closed the box, holding it still as she sealed it with packing tape, and tried to push back the sadness that always threatened when she thought of her late husband.

He'd loved the Marines, and had signed up for a third tour, even though Olivia had begged him to get out so they could settle down and raise their family together.

But sure enough, no sooner had he re-enlisted than he'd been deployed.

Not anywhere exceptionally dangerous, but during a training exercise, he'd been killed, and he'd never gotten to go to Okinawa.

She had been planning on going with him, and while all of her was devastated that she had lost her husband, there was a part of her that was happy that she hadn't had to move across the globe into a country that she had no interest in making her home.

Japan was probably a really amazing country, and she wouldn't mind visiting, but she didn't want to live there. She wanted to live right here in Mistletoe Meadows. Except... she wanted to live here with her husband and children, not as a single mom and a grieving widow.

Cam, why didn't you listen to me?

She wanted to scream it in his face, although it would do no good. He'd just laugh and ruffle her hair like she was two instead of thirty, and tell her that she was worrying for nothing.

It was so annoying. Because she'd been right. She wasn't worrying for nothing. She was worrying because it was legit to worry, and her fears had come true. And now, their boys, Aiden and Ethan, were four years old and had no memories of their father. Cam hadn't even known she was expecting when he had died.

She was still upset about the fact that he had re-enlisted, and she hadn't told him what she suspected.

Plus, she'd been scared. She didn't want to have babies over on the other side of the world.

Well, she didn't have to. She had them at home, and she had them alone.

Swallowing, she noticed the headlights flash across the shop, and looked out the window to see that the new pastor had arrived at the parsonage for the last time. Mrs. Tucker had said that he had one more load, and then he'd be there for good. That was when Mrs. Tucker had picked up the candle that Olivia always gave anyone moving to the community as a housewarming gift. It smelled like freshly made bread, and she could just sit and burn it all day long. She loved the scent, and was kind of proud of herself for coming up with it. It was one that she had invented back when candles were still a hobby for her. Something she did as therapy, to fill the long days and nights when her husband wasn't home.

She had never aspired to be more than a wife and a mother. It's what she'd always wanted. Well, she did enjoy leading her small Bible studies, and was working on writing one for herself. Not that she ever thought she would publish it. She just always had ideas and thoughts about God and reading the Bible, and had decided to organize them in a way that she could go back and look at years from now. Plus, she took copious sermon notes, and had notebooks full of those things too. That was her other hobby. But... what was that to a dead Marine's wife?

She'd kind of gotten away from that in recent years, because partly the candle shop had taken all of her time, and partly because she was a little angry at God. How could he give her twins, and then take her husband away almost in the same breath?

Were those the actions of a loving God? She didn't think so. How could she say that God was good, when she wasn't even sure she believed that anymore?

The car lights shut off, plunging the entire area into darkness. And then she saw the light flicker.

Mrs. Tucker must have lit the candle and put it somewhere in the parsonage.

That made Olivia smile. The idea that there would be a little welcome for the pastor. A little smell of freshly made bread, and maybe it would make him smile.

She hadn't met him. The twins had been sick for a month earlier that fall when he had come for several Sundays and pastored the congregation as a candidate for the church.

Apparently the congregation hadn't needed to hear anyone else, because they loved this Pastor Mark Stevens so much.

Plus he was a good friend of Noah Parker.

As much as Olivia loved Noah, and admired and respected him, she would've liked to have heard the pastor for herself.

But she couldn't take her sick children to church, and one of the things that a single mother didn't have the luxury of doing was to discuss with her husband which one of them was going to go and which one of them was going to stay.

Everything was on her shoulders.

She set the box aside and started packing a new one. She had twenty more orders to do before she could quit for the night.

Her eyes were drawn again to the window, just in time to see the lights in the parsonage go on, and see a figure, tall and broad-shouldered, outlined in the door before it closed behind him.

She hadn't even asked how old the pastor was, although someone had told her that he was a single man with no children. That made her feel like maybe he was just a kid out of college. That age felt so long ago for her. She had been so young and full of dreams and so sure that she could conquer the world, and then she'd met Cam and fallen in love and been eager to start their lives together.

None of it had turned out the way she thought.

She carefully put a brochure at the top of the box before she closed it and grabbed the packing tape again.

Leaning over, she punched the button on her computer to send the information to the printer to print out a label.

She used to love making candles and packing them with care, sending them along to brighten someone's day - literally. But now that she had to do it in order to feed her family, it felt more like pressure, less like fun.

She supposed that's what being an adult was.

There was rustling from the back, and she turned her head, glancing at her boys.

At four years old, they only had one more year at home with her before she had to send them to kindergarten.

In her mind, when she got married, she had wanted to homeschool. But there was just no way she could take the time that would entail and still work full-time to support the family.

Lord, I know I have to give up things that I want in order to do your will. But when they're good things, things that I think should be your will, but seem to not be, it's hard.

Wouldn't it be best for the boys to be homeschooled? For her to keep them out of school and teach them from God's word every day, showing them science and history from the lens of a Christian perspective?

She wouldn't say that she was bitter against God, but she definitely wasn't as close to Him as she used to be. After all, she didn't really understand why he'd taken her husband and left her alone.

Maybe it was so that she would reconcile with her parents.

No. She wasn't even going to go there. She wouldn't even entertain that thought.

"Mommy?" Aiden, the more outgoing and energetic of the two boys, came out of the back room, rubbing his eyes. "Is it time to go home?"

"As soon as I get these orders packed," she said gently.

Aiden looked so much like his dad. Blonde hair, blue eyes, a mischievous grin, and a bent towards trouble.

Ethan was so much more like her, dark and serious, always counting the cost before he jumped in behind his twin.

They got along so well, since Aiden was the natural leader and Ethan was his natural sidekick. Of course, Ethan had a tendency to think things through, and as the boys had gotten older, she noticed Aiden depending more and more on his twin's ability to process information. It was how she and Cam had worked.

A scraping sound pulled her mind back to the present. Aiden had gotten his stool and was sliding it over. He climbed up, got the curly paper ribbons that she boxed up with the candles, and started putting them in the bottom of the open box beside her.

"With your help I'll get done a lot sooner."

He grinned up at her. "Ethan's still sleeping."

"He is. It was really good of you to get up without waking him."

"That's what you told me to do," he chirped, already his naturally optimistic and positive personality coming out.

"Yeah." When he was younger, he'd had a tendency to run over everything, with no concept that there were other people in the world. That included his brother, who always required a little bit more sleep. Aiden would wake him up without meaning to, and then she would have two grumpy boys on her hands.

Those days of juggling the twins were so hard.

They wouldn't have been that hard if you would've allowed your parents to help you.

She finished wrapping the candle in crinkly paper and pulled the ends down, nestling it into the curly cues Aiden had put in the bottom. She was not going to think about her parents, and was not going to think about Cam.

She could think about the new pastor, and wonder what changes he would bring. Everyone at the church hoped that he'd pretty much keep everything the same, since Pastor Johnson had been so beloved by everyone. But she knew that a new person usually liked to put their mark on things.

Hopefully he wouldn't go and mess up a bunch of stuff that was already working.

Hopefully, he would like her candles, and not go to the church meeting later this week and tell them that he wanted to cancel the tradition. She was depending on that order since she made almost fifty percent of her income in December, and a good chunk of that was the church orders she fulfilled.

Looking back, maybe Pastor Johnson had ordered more candles than strictly necessary just to support her and enable her to work.

She hated accepting help from anyone, and while she didn't think that she was proud of the fact that she was able to do things on her own, she definitely did like that she had been able to support herself. Without depending on the government, or anyone else, to take care of her.

That was especially true considering that she didn't have a college education, and almost everyone had assumed that she was going to go crawling back to her parents once her husband died.

She supposed she'd proved those people wrong.

But even as she thought that, she knew that it wasn't just her. God had been good to her. She really couldn't take credit for any of it.

"This is the last one?" Aidan piped up from beside her.

He slid the last box that she had out on the table and started filling it.

"It sure is. The work just flew by with you helping me."

He beamed. Both of her boys loved helping, and she was glad they did, since so much of their time was spent in the shop, trying to make enough candles that she could keep food on the table and the lights on.

So far, so good.

Chapter Three

$\mathcal{M}$ark stood at the door of the vestibule, greeting the folks of Mistletoe Meadows as they filed in.

Pastor Johnson had gone to Mexico for Christmas, visiting his son who was a missionary in Guadalajara and ran an orphanage there.

It was the first Christmas he was going to get to spend with his son in twenty years. And it was the first Christmas in forty that he wouldn't be here with the folks at Mistletoe Meadows.

"Welcome. I'm so glad you could come today," he said as he shook an older fellow's hand. He couldn't remember the man's name. There was no way that he could possibly remember all the people's names that he had met the two times that he had preached sermons here earlier this year. He must've met a hundred people and he wasn't that great with names to begin with.

"I'm here every Sunday," the man said, like he should know that.

"It's always good to be in the house of the Lord," he said, hoping that was a sufficiently innocent response.

That was another thing. Some people had gone to church especially because they knew that a new person would be preaching.

He didn't know who were regulars, there every time the doors opened, and who were people who had just shown up out of curiosity.

He supposed those were things that he would learn, and not that it mattered. God was not a respecter of persons, and he shouldn't be either.

"I'm so excited to hear your sermon today. I've been looking forward to this day, and I've been praying for you since we knew you were being hired. And even before that, I just prayed that God would allow his plan to unfold, and we wouldn't get in the way."

Marjorie McBride, a lady who had definitely made an impression on him when he was here before, stood in the doorway, beaming at him like she was his mother and he was her only son.

Her warm handshake made him feel relaxed and like someone was in his corner.

"You're looking better," he said simply. He'd known for a while that Marjorie McBride had not been well. His church was just forty-five minutes away, and Marjorie McBride's influence had spread all over the mountain. He doubted that there were too many people who didn't know who she was, or that she had been fighting leukemia for years.

"I think my body is finally starting to get victory over the cancer. I'm not sure if it's the natural remedies I'm taking, or if it's prayer. I'd say a little of both," she said, truly looking happy and content. Peaceful. Like she would've been okay with dying, but she was happy to live too.

"I've gotta say I'm happy that they're working, because from what Pastor Johnson has told me, this church and community really need you."

"I'm here to do God's will for as long as he'll have me here."

She filed in, and he continued to greet people, including Marjorie's children, until the piano started playing and it was time for him to go to the front.

They were blessed to have Noah, who owned the music shop in

town, and his wife, providing such good music to encourage the congregation to look to the Lord before the service even started.

At his old church they had sung a cappella, because they hadn't had anyone to play an instrument for them. He could draw out a few chords on the guitar, and sometimes he tried to do that, but sometimes he was so bad that he wasn't sure whether his playing made the singing worse or better. Over the years, he'd become more proficient, but they eventually had someone who could play the piano come in.

He could've used piped music—a lot of churches did—but it just didn't have the same personal touch as having someone play an instrument as the congregation sang. Plus, if he wanted to sing the chorus again or skip a verse, canned music made it hard.

Regardless, he was sure to appreciate the music, after not having it for so many years.

Was that your plan all along, Lord? To give me an appreciation for the things that I have, by taking them away for a while?

Maybe he would appreciate his wife even more, because he'd spent so many years without one.

He wanted to remind God that he was still waiting, and that he would appreciate her, but the music stopped and it was time for him to step up to the front.

His hands sweated and his heart thundered. He didn't know why —they had already hired him, and it wasn't like he had to worry about the impression he made. But he didn't want them to regret their choice. He wanted them to feel that they had made the right decision in hiring him.

The church was packed, although Pastor Johnson had said it usually was. He had talked about building a new building, but he had felt that that was a baton best handed to a new and younger person.

He greeted the congregation, went through the announcements without incident, and began his sermon.

"And so yesterday when I was sitting in my car, feeling a little lonely, and like the world was cold and dark, I looked up, and I saw the light shining in the window. It was warm and it flickered in a warm and welcoming way, and it gave off a beautiful scent that when I opened my door, smelled like fresh-baked bread. It made walking into my house and coming home feel good instead of like I was lost and alone. That's how Christians can be to the lost. We can guide them to where they need to go, we can show them the way so they don't get lost or drift, and they can hear—"

That's when the microphone cut out.

Suddenly, he felt like he was speaking into a void.

"Okay, I guess that was perfect timing." The people in the front chuckled, since the folks in the back couldn't hear him.

The sound person was frantically working, and Mark knew there was no point in trying to rush him. It wasn't his fault. Things happened. And God was in control all the time. Although, he felt like his sermon was building towards a very good climax, and he didn't really understand why God would allow the microphone to cut out and all the momentum that he'd been building toward the altar call be lost.

"So you know how students will sometimes test their teachers by putting pinecones on their seat or doing some other mischievous thing," he said, referring to the old movies. He'd spoken in his loudest voice, and he saw grins on a lot of faces. "So did someone do this on purpose just to initiate me into my new position?"

There was laughter all around, and then he said, "My dad always said that I had the booming voice of a preacher, even from the youngest age, so I don't think I need a microphone."

"I think I have it fixed!" The sound guy, sweat beading his brow, looked hopefully at the front.

"Testing, testing, one, two, three," he said. Then he tapped the microphone. It echoed through the church.

"Can you hear me now?" he asked, and the congregation laughed again.

He'd lost the thread of the sermon, but he did have people

smiling, and he felt like even though it probably did take some of the wind out of the sails of his message, laughter and navigating bumps and bobbles helped people to feel united. Maybe that was what the Lord was about. Or maybe it was something that he couldn't figure out today, but he'd know a decade from now. Whatever it was, he figured there was nothing to do but get back into his sermon, and so that's what he did. Things like that, that he had no control over, he had to assume that God would use for his good and God's glory, since that was God's promise.

He was able to launch back into his sermon without too much trouble. Things felt like they were going pretty well when he noticed movement in the back.

A woman, a young boy on either side of her, slipped in without making a sound. There was space in the back pew, and she got her boys there quickly and silently, like they'd done that multiple times before. Her hair looked a little messed, and she wore some kind of apron over top of her jeans and sweatshirt, like she'd been working that morning and had forgotten to take her apron off. It wasn't an apron like she had been baking, but more like she'd been working with... oil? He wasn't sure, but both boys looked a little sleepy, with one of them having their hair sticking almost straight up.

He knew that a lot of people would judge if someone came to church looking less than perfect, but his philosophy had always been that he appreciated having people make the time to come, and the harder it was for them to get there, the more it didn't matter what they looked like when they arrived. It looked to him like that woman had deliberately made time, when she really didn't have it, to be in the house of the Lord that morning.

All of those things ran through his mind while he continued with the sermon. He was always on the lookout to see if any of his congregants had any special needs, or things that he could help with. That woman seemed like a prime candidate for something, although he would have to get to know her a little better to figure out what. He also wondered where her husband was. Maybe he was unsaved, and it was up to the woman to get herself and her children ready for church in the morning. Maybe she had to finish her work up in order to keep her husband happy before she could come.

There were a lot of people that morning that he made a little mental note about, and that woman was one. He wanted to find out more about her, and see if there was anything he could do to help. After all, it was not just his job to deliver a sermon on Sunday morning, but it was his job to shepherd the flock as best he was able. Getting to know them, and figuring out how he could help enabled him to be the hands and feet of Jesus.

He was eager to get started.

Chapter Four

*M*onday morning, Olivia was in the back of the candle shop, making candles to replenish her stock for the Christmas season.

She almost started on the special order the church usually put in for Christmas Eve, but with the new pastor, she wasn't sure that the standing order Pastor Johnson had would hold.

She had liked the pastor well enough the day before, what little she'd heard of the sermon. She had gotten up early so she could get some more work in before she went to church, and then ended up realizing that she had more to do than what she thought, and hurried to get as much done as she could. She hadn't left enough time to get herself and the twins ready, and she had been sitting in the service for fifteen minutes before she realized she had come with her apron and not her coat.

At least she had shoes on. And the kids did too. One Sunday she had shown up with both of her children, but only one of them had shoes.

Still, she hadn't had a chance to talk to the pastor, since he had been surrounded by people once the service was over and she needed to get downstairs because she taught Sunday school and needed to be in her classroom.

She was sure she would be introduced to the pastor at some point, and hoped that she would have enough presence about her to ask about the candle order.

She didn't want to sound desperate, but she also needed to know if she needed to sell more candles some other way, or whether she could depend on the church to be business as usual.

"Mommy? Is it almost time for lunch?"

She looked down at Aiden. The kid seemed to always be hungry. Ethan, on the other hand, had to be coaxed to eat sometimes.

It showed in their physiques too, with Aiden being husky and with chubby baby cheeks, while Ethan was slightly slimmer and just looked a little less healthy to her.

Not that he was sick all the time—far from it—but as a mom, she worried a bit. She really couldn't afford for either one of them to get sick anyway. Or herself. An ounce of prevention was worth a pound of cure in that regard, so she tried to be careful.

"I just have about forty-five minutes more work to do. You two can get the crackers that are on the shelf behind you, and you can munch on them while you're playing with your trucks on the floor if you'd like."

He nodded eagerly, and then ran to the shelf to grab the crackers.

She didn't like to let her kids eat too many snacks, but sometimes when she was working, she didn't have a choice.

The bell rang, indicating someone had stepped into the shop. She was open, but didn't typically have too many customers this early in the morning, so she didn't hesitate to work in the back room.

She couldn't see the door from where she stood, so she just called, "Go ahead and look around. I'll be out in a minute!"

There were footsteps, and then a voice made her glance up.

"If it's okay, I actually came to talk to you. I'll just stand here?"

It took her a moment to recognize the new pastor. He looked a little different when he wasn't wearing a suit and tie. He had on jeans and a sweatshirt and looked very casual. More casual than Pastor Johnson ever did.

"Did Mrs. Tucker approve that outfit?"

She could've slapped a hand over her mouth after she said that. Maybe the new pastor didn't have a sense of humor.

But he laughed. "She does have a lot to say about what goes on in the church, and I'm guessing she has just as much to say about what goes on in the town. But I could be wrong."

"No, you're exactly right. She's a great lady, though. She watches my children on occasion, and is always first in line to cook a meal if we're under the weather. I love her, but I'm pretty sure she would shake her head at what you're wearing right now."

"I see. Well, maybe I'll have to talk with her and explain that my wardrobe might not be up to her standards."

"You can do so at your own peril," she said with an exaggerated shudder.

She really did love Mrs. Tucker to death, and didn't mean anything unkind. Mrs. Tucker would be the first to say that she liked to see people dress in what she called an old-fashioned way, where they were still fairly formal for today's society.

"She gave me a little bit of grief when she saw that I had worn jeans to church on Sunday, and I guess it's a good thing I realized I wore my apron and got it removed before she saw me, or I might've gotten in trouble for that too."

"I saw you in your apron. So now I have blackmail material I can hold over your head. I think I'll tuck that in my back pocket for when I might need it."

She looked up at him, her mouth open, and then realized he was joking. But it was still a little shocking, since he was a pastor. She wasn't used to a pastor having a sense of humor.

"All right, I'll remember that and watch my p's and q's around you."

She straightened out the wick, and then said, "Is it okay if I continue to work while we talk?"

"Sure. I didn't want to interrupt you. But I saw you come into church... Although I didn't know it was you until you mentioned wearing your apron. Then I put the two together."

"I guess I made quite a first impression," she said, laughing to herself a bit. Of course he remembered the person who came in late wearing a work apron.

"Twins, right?" He nodded at the boys playing on the floor in the corner. They were used to people coming in and out of the shop, and Aiden especially could be quite friendly. But other times they didn't even notice where there were people around.

"Yes. They're four."

"Does your husband work in the shop too?"

She blinked, looking at her hands holding the wick without really seeing it.

She took a breath and looked up. "My husband was a marine who was killed in a training accident before he even knew I was pregnant with the twins."

"I see. I'm sorry for your loss."

"Yeah. I am too. Sometimes I wonder what in the world God is thinking. Actually, sometimes I have a hard time forgiving the Lord for allowing that to happen to me. You know? He's supposed to be good. Leaving two little boys to grow up without their father doesn't seem to be very good to me."

She had lowered her voice so her boys wouldn't hear her talking like that. She didn't want them to be mad at God. She didn't want them to blame Him either, although... who else was there to blame? If God really was all powerful, then he could've kept Cam from dying. And he didn't.

There was no other way to look at that other than that was not good.

"I've found that sometimes the things I think are the worst things that could possibly happen to me turn out to be some of the best. Not to belittle or make insignificant your loss. Just more of a defense of God, I guess."

"Yeah. You can defend God if you want to. I suppose He deserves it, but I guess there's just no way you can look me straight in the eye and tell me that those boys should not have a dad."

"Of course I wouldn't say that. But there are instances all through the Bible where bad things happen, and God worked good out of them. I guess the first thing that comes to mind is David and Bathsheba. That was a really, really bad thing. No one could say that adultery was good. That murder is good. And yet, Bathsheba was the mother of Solomon, who was the wisest man who ever lived. So God did work good out of it. It just wasn't the way we thought it should look, you know?"

She didn't say anything. She could definitely relate to Bathsheba, losing her husband in war no less. Although, Cam had not been deliberately killed. It had been an accident, no question. She looked down. He couldn't have chosen a better, more relatable story.

"So where do you think the good has happened?" she asked, working a little more slowly than she normally did, because she was thinking too. Had she missed an angle?

"I don't know. Your story isn't over yet, is it?"

"No, I suppose it's not. But isn't it best for a child to have both mother and father?"

"And maybe there will be a father in the picture at some point."

"Well, he's gonna have to come here and court me here, because I don't have time to go running around trying to find someone."

"Maybe you'll find someone at church."

"Hardly. There really aren't any eligible men under sixty. And... I'm not robbing the nursing home just to give my kids a dad."

Chapter Five

Mark stood still. It was on the tip of his tongue to say that he was available, eligible, and unmarried, but... he wasn't trying to come on to her in any way. He had just come to visit her as one of his congregants. He'd also been told that he needed to talk to her about the candles for the candlelight service. And then somehow they got to talking about marriage and men and who was eligible in the church, and there was a part of him that was inside, jumping up and down with his hand raised, shouting, "Me, me!" But... that was part of the problem. It was like a teacher marrying a student. He couldn't court someone in his congregation. He was supposed to be their shepherd, not their lover.

Plus, he wanted to marry someone who was interested in helping him with the church. It was a huge responsibility, and churches normally expected the pastor's wife to run Bible studies and organize meals for shut-ins and sick people, and pitch in wherever she can, and he would hope that she would go along on visitation with him, particularly if he were visiting ladies in the hospital, and to console wives and mothers alongside him. To be his helpmate.

This lady was obviously a business owner.

"I suppose you already know I'm Mark Stevens. It's good to meet you," he said, holding his hand out and realizing belatedly he didn't even know her name.

"My name is Olivia Winters. And it's good to meet you too. Nice change of subject, by the way," she said, laughing a little, like he'd done it on purpose. Maybe he had. He was feeling a little spooked, and didn't know what to say, because there technically was an eligible man in the church now.

"It's not easy to be a business owner," he said, not really digging for information, but just trying to get to know her a little.

"It wasn't my plan. But I guess we've already established the fact that I'm bitter against God and I shouldn't be."

"It wasn't your plan?" he asked, ignoring what she said about being bitter. He couldn't blame her. He didn't understand why God moved the way He did, worked the way He did, or why some people suffered tragedy after tragedy while it seemed like others led a charmed life. He couldn't say that he thought it was fair. And he definitely couldn't say that she shouldn't be bitter. He knew that she shouldn't, but he had no right to tell her. He hadn't lost a spouse.

"No. This was just a hobby. I love it. I really love coming up with different scents."

"The baked bread scent that you gave me was amazing. I was totally fooled into thinking that there was warm, homemade bread with melted butter on it somewhere in my house, but alas, it was just a candle."

"Sorry to disappoint you," she said with a chuckle.

"I wasn't disappointed. It was very welcoming. I don't think you could've picked a better one."

"Thanks. That's what I love to send, especially if I know it's going to be lit before people get there. There's nothing like warm baked bread, is there?"

"No. Definitely made the house feel welcoming. You're very good at it, like I said."

"Thanks. I think sometimes when things stop being a hobby and start being something that you have to depend on in order for your livelihood, you have a tendency to... maybe not enjoy them as much."

"I see. So you work because you have to, not because you want to?"

"I'm blessed to be able to do something I love. But... I guess this wasn't exactly my dream." She lifted a shoulder and went back to work, looking at her hands, and while he was curious as to what her dream actually was, he wasn't sure it was something she wanted to talk about.

"I actually was here on a little bit of business."

"Okay," she said, glancing up and seeming interested.

"Mrs. Tucker told me that you typically provide special order candles for the church. That does have to be approved by the church committee, but I figured I would just drop in and check to make sure that we were still on the same page."

"I was wondering that myself. Pastor Johnson has been very generous to me. I'm sure part of it was that he wanted to support the single mom with twin boys who was trying to make a living, and part of it is because the candles really were a huge asset to the church. They lit them on Christmas Eve, and then used them almost the entire month of January. Some services they did entirely by candlelight. It makes January a much cozier, happier month."

"I would imagine it would. Pastor Johnson gave me a heads up on a lot of things, but he hadn't mentioned that."

"I'm sure there were much more important things he needed to talk about."

"So you're still able to provide the candles as you normally do?"

"Yes. I haven't started making them yet, because I wasn't sure where we were. I also know that the church was trying to cut the budget in some areas so they could send more money to missions this year, and I wasn't sure whether the candles, which are an extra, unnecessary, expense, were on the chopping block or not."

"The meeting is tomorrow. I should be able to tell you by Wednesday at the very latest."

"That'll be fine. I have plenty of time to make them. They are always a labor of love."

She seemed happy and content, and not pressured at all. Although, she did seem to work an awful lot. He'd noticed her light on until late in the night the night before, even though it was Sunday.

"Your shop is not open on Sunday, but you still worked."

"I did. I know we're supposed to take a day of rest, but this time of year, I need to do everything I can, because the sales from the Christmas season make up almost half of my budget for the year."

"Wow. That's a lot."

"Yeah. So you can see why I might work seven days a week just to make sure that I can stay solvent the rest of the year. I try not to make it a habit."

"I'm glad to hear that. Everyone needs rest."

"You work on Sundays."

Her voice sounded reasonable and conversational, not accusatory. She wasn't trying to do a gotcha on him. At least he didn't get that impression.

"But I take another day of the week off. Usually Tuesday or Thursday. But I'll settle into a schedule here."

"Your previous pastorate wasn't that far away, was it?"

"No. It wasn't."

He wondered why Noah had never mentioned Olivia as someone the Secret Saint could help. He had been helping Noah Parker with Secret Saint activities for more than a year. Almost two years. It was a fun thing that someone in Mistletoe Meadows had started, and they had passed the baton around until there was a huge network of people who told other people who told other people about anyone who might need anything. The town was practically famous for their Secret Saint tradition every Christmas. But to his knowledge Olivia's name had never come up.

"I imagine your parents probably help you a good bit with the children."

"No. I haven't talked to my parents in more than four years."

Wow. There was something going on there. As a pastor, he wanted to probe a little deeper, but he had just met her, and he thought that maybe he should let it rest. Maybe he would hear bits and pieces from someone else, not that he wanted to gossip. But her mouth pressed down tight and she was more absorbed in her work than she had been since he arrived. She obviously did not want to talk about it.

"My parents passed away about that long ago. I miss them dreadfully."

"I'm sorry. I guess you would've lost them just shortly before I lost my husband."

No husband, and she didn't talk to her parents. Interesting.

"Well, it was good to meet you. I'm going around trying to meet everyone, and I did have a little piece of business to deal with you, but it sounds like we're on for the candles as long as everything goes well at the meeting tomorrow."

"That's right. If there's anything else that you need in the meantime, you can let me know."

"I'm sorry I missed you yesterday at church."

"After the service I had to go down because I teach Sunday school to the three- and four-year-olds. But you seemed to be swarmed anyway, and I figured there would be plenty of time for us to meet. I didn't realize you were going to be showing up at my shop today."

So that's why he hadn't seen her. She taught Sunday school. Interesting.

There was a little voice in the back of his head that said that was what a good pastor's wife would do, but he tried to shut it down. This woman had a lot of baggage, from her anger at God, to the fact that she didn't talk to her parents, to trying to keep a business afloat by herself.

"Well, if you need me, you know where I'll be. The door swings both ways."

She looked up at his saying and smiled, like she hadn't heard it in a while but liked it.

He returned her smile, nodded, and then turned to leave with a last glance at the boys. They were cute, and had been playing nicely together the whole time he had been visiting. Obviously, they were used to being in the shop when she was with customers.

"Hey, mister," one of the boys said, looking up and catching him looking at them.

"Hey there. Looks like you guys have a nice collection of trucks."

He glanced at Olivia and raised his brows. She looked over his shoulder and nodded in answer to his unspoken question.

He walked over and hunched down.

"What are you hauling?" he asked, pointing to the truck that was parked at his feet.

"That one has potatoes on it. And that one has candles," the boy said.

The other boy didn't say much, but nodded along with his brother. It made sense that one of the boys was a little more outgoing than the other. In his experience, that was often true of siblings, where the ones that hung back were able to because there were others that stepped forward to talk.

Family dynamics had always been interesting to him, and twins were especially intriguing.

"Are you the new pastor?" the little boy who hadn't said anything yet asked.

"I am. I'm Pastor Mark. What's your name?" He held his hand out to the little boy who had asked.

"I'm Ethan." The boy looked at his hand, as though he weren't used to shaking adults' hands, and then his little hand came out and slipped into Mark's much larger one.

He shook it solemnly, and then looked at the other little boy.

"I'm Pastor Mark. Who are you?" he asked, offering him a handshake as well.

This boy smiled confidently and grabbed Pastor Mark's hand like he'd shaken a million of them before in his life. "I'm Aiden. It's very nice to meet you."

He sounded like a little adult, like he was parroting something his mother or another adult had said.

"The feeling is mutual," Mark said, biting back a grin.

"Do you want to play with us?" Ethan said, looking eager.

"No, dummy. Don't ask him to play with us. If he stays, Mom's never gonna have lunch ready."

Mark laughed at Aiden trying to whisper to his brother.

"I'd love to play with you guys, but maybe some other time. I have some other visits I need to make today."

"That's your job?" Aidan asked. Apparently it was okay for him to talk to the pastor—it was just Ethan who got in trouble.

"It actually is. It's my job to go around and visit people, and to talk to them about Jesus, or anything else they want to talk about. And to see how I can help them."

"And you get paid for that?" Ethan said, his eyes wide.

Mark chuckled. "It's pretty amazing, isn't it?" He almost went into how he worked for God and not for man, but while the kids seemed to be pretty intelligent for four-year-olds, he didn't want to hold up their lunch any longer than necessary. In fact, he was getting a little hungry himself. "I won't hold you up anymore. Maybe Mom will get lunch on the table if I scoot out of here."

"I'm hungry," Aidan said in a little voice that mimicked his own.

"I bet you are. Although, you don't have to take a nap after lunch, do you?"

"Not if Mom doesn't remember," Aiden said, looking at his mom over Mark's shoulder, as though he were hoping that she didn't hear him.

"All right. Well, have a good day, and hopefully no naps."

The boys waved bye and went back to their playing as Mark straightened and walked toward the door into the shop.

"Nice kids," he said. Meaning it. They were mature for their age, and polite, although still children, and still human.

"Thanks. You're good with them," Olivia said, and his heart warmed. He didn't think he was particularly great with children, but Olivia's compliment seemed sincere, and he'd take it.

"Thanks." He couldn't think of anything else to say, and really did have a couple of other visits he wanted to make. A few other items of business he wanted to get settled before he went to the meeting the next night.

"Take care. I'm sure I'll see you around. Thanks for chatting with me today."

"No problem. See ya."

There was a lot about Olivia that intrigued him, and he hoped that he would continue to get to know her.

Chapter Six

The clanging of bells as the children's bell choir practiced downstairs with Noah gave the church meeting room a festive, happy holiday vibe, as if the wreaths hanging over the crosses weren't enough.

Mark glanced around at the chairs that had been arranged in a circle. Mrs. Tucker was busy bustling around getting everything ready and welcoming everyone, like she was the self-appointed greeter.

Maybe there was some rule that said that she was supposed to greet everyone. Mark really didn't know. This was his first ever church meeting here in Mistletoe Meadows.

It had felt like a whirlwind since he had started, with him trying to make sure that he was able to visit every member of his congregation, and not just for his new position as pastor.

He might as well use what he had been given to make sure that everyone was well taken care of for Christmas, because with his Secret Saint activities, he had more avenues of finding out who needed help.

Immediately, Olivia came to mind. But what could he do for her?

He glanced down at the agenda that Mrs. Tucker had passed out. Number one was talking about the candles for the Christmas Eve candlelight service.

From what he understood, Pastor Johnson had always gotten the candles from Olivia, and now he wondered if maybe that wasn't because Pastor Johnson knew that Olivia could use the money. And she was too proud to ask for help, or even accept it.

"Everyone's here. You can call the meeting to order. Noah will slip in after all of the children have left his music class. But it's not supposed to end for another fifteen minutes or so." Mrs. Tucker smiled at him, speaking in a low voice, like they were conspiring together.

He nodded his head, and even though Mrs. Tucker seemed like she could be an overbearing kind of person, he appreciated her organization and the energy that she put into helping. So many churches had a ton of members, but only a few who actually did anything to help the church.

People were busy with their lives, and he didn't resent that. But he certainly wasn't going to be upset because someone wanted to help and was a little bit pushy about doing it. He would be grateful for what God had given him.

Thank you, Lord, for people like Mrs. Tucker who make my job easier and are willing to do things that no one else will do. And enable me to do my job.

Like visiting each member of his congregation with the eye of a shepherd.

He glanced around the chairs, and then took his own seat, holding the paper in his hand underneath his Bible.

"Welcome to the committee meeting. I'm so glad you all could make it."

There were some murmurs and someone mentioned about it being his first meeting.

He grinned. "I know. And I suppose it's always wise to begin as you mean to go on. That's why we're gonna start out with prayer and a short passage of scripture. I promise I'm not going to preach."

"Go ahead and preach. That's what we hired you for," one of the McBride boys said. There were a bunch of them, and he hadn't quite gotten them all figured out yet.

He'd talked to them on more than one occasion, even before he was the pastor. They were the movers and the shakers in the town, and he appreciated knowing that many of them were also involved in the church, enough so that they were here on a weeknight for a committee meeting.

He bowed his head and took a moment to gather his thoughts. His heart was overflowing, and he knew God knew that. He also knew that God knew he was intimidated by the great task before him. This church was much bigger, much more active, and the town was too, than his last. Where his last church felt intimate and like a family, this hadn't quite gotten into that feeling for him yet.

Lord God, please be with us this evening as we move forward with the work of your church. Help us to remember that it's your church. Thank you for each and every one that's gathered here tonight. Thank you that they've left the tasks that could so easily take their attention away from you, in order to be here, to help in your house. Please give each one who came tonight an extra special blessing for showing up and making your work a priority in their lives. Help us to remember that everything we do should be a reflection of Jesus, and help us to do what you would have us to do, and not think that we're doing this in our own flesh, but rather in your strength. Amen.

He looked up at the people who were looking at him expectantly, and then he took a breath as he opened his Bible to the page that he had marked.

"Let everything be done decently and in order," he read simply, before he closed his Bible and looked around the circle. He grinned a bit. "That just seemed like a really good verse to start out my first meeting in my new church. I've heard stories about other churches, not this one, where committee meetings have degenerated into screaming contests, and I've even heard of chairs being tossed, along with hymnbooks." He took a moment to laugh along with everyone else. The possibility of that happening seemed remote and far away, but he was pretty sure that the church where it had happened hadn't been intending to throw anything either. The human heart was wicked, and he supposed each person here could be surprised at the depths of depravity to which they could sink if they were given that opportunity. He didn't plan on the opportunity presenting itself.

"I think as long as we remember that we're to treat other people the way we want to be treated—it's like Jesus said - that's the rule that underlines everything. We put God first, and that is all we need to do. Love God, love each other. And then, the decently and in order will happen automatically. But the loving others doesn't usually happen unless we specifically make it so."

There were a few nods around the circle, and then he reached around and set his Bible on the table behind him.

"That's all I have to say. I don't want to take up a whole lot of your time, but I do think every meeting should start with prayer and a little bit of Bible, with a bit of commentary from me. After all, like Mr. McBride said, that's what you hired me for."

There were some murmurs and a couple of chuckles, and then he lifted up the paper.

"All right. Number one on this paper says that we're going to talk about the Christmas Eve service, and most importantly, the candles for it."

"Good candles make the service," Mrs. Tucker said.

Mark gave her a thoughtful look. It sounded like she was on the side of spending a little more for Olivia's candles.

"We've got to cut the budget somewhere," Bob Knapp said. He was an older gentleman, and the kind of person who looked like he believed frugality was next to godliness.

"I do agree, we should not squander our resources, but use them prayerfully and well," Mark said, not wanting to antagonize anyone, and also not wanting to argue. Perhaps he also wanted to give the other side a point before he tried to convince them that his way was wise.

"Pastor Johnson always wanted to get the candles from Olivia, because he said she needed the money. I guess I'm just wondering how long she's going to need the money. Shouldn't she be able to have her business support itself?"

"When I lost my husband, I didn't know how I was going to survive. I was in a bad way for a long time," Mrs. Tucker said, and her words were not antagonistic. She was just sharing.

Mark had heard some about what Mrs. Tucker had done, stealing from the church in order to make ends meet. No one had realized how bad off she was, because she was too proud to let anyone know. That, or she didn't want to complain. Maybe Mark should give her the benefit of the doubt. Regardless, everyone nodded and looked sober. No one wanted anyone to be reduced to stealing in order to put food in their mouth.

"If my son hadn't come to live with me, I don't know what I would've done," Mrs. Tucker continued, her face serious and her tone conversational. Not accusatory. "I just feel like the Bible truly commands us to take care of widows."

Mark quoted the verse. "Pure religion and undefiled before God and the Father is this, to visit the fatherless and widows in their affliction, and to keep himself unspotted from the world."

"That's impressive, Pastor. Do you have a lot of verses memorized?" Ralph Jones, who had been quiet up to that point, asked.

"Not as many as I would like to. I know people who have entire books memorized. I don't have that, not even any of the shorter ones, like Jude."

"Still, to be able to call up a verse to make your point is better than having any kind of argument," Ralph continued.

Millie Sanderson nodded. "We can argue with you, but we can't argue with the Bible."

"All right, I'm not sure what that means, though. I've heard that

Olivia's candles are the highest quality, and that many times the church has used them to burn throughout January, which is typically a dark month. I've heard they brighten the church and encourage people to come. Not to mention, her scents are delicate and lovely, but not overpowering where people who are allergic are unable to handle them."

It was true, Pastor Johnson had gone on and on about Olivia's candles. But mostly, he'd said that Olivia needed to work, and then Pastor Johnson had quoted the verse about taking care of widows. Then he'd said sometimes you just had to make a person feel like they were contributing to society, and not like they were a charity case.

Mark figured Pastor Johnson's wisdom far surpassed his own, and he thought it was a good idea, not just to support someone in their congregation, but to help a widow in her time of need, and also to purchase something from her, and not just throw money at her like charity. Although there wasn't anything wrong with charity.

"The church can use the extra money that we would save on purchasing cheaper candles on other things that would be beneficial to the community," Bob Knapp spoke up. "We could just give Olivia money if she needed it. Has she asked for it?"

"I think it would be better to purchase something from her business, to support her that way, rather than just throwing money at her." Thankfully, when Ralph Jones spoke, he didn't seem like he was attacking Bob's point of view, just disagreeing with it casually.

"I agree with that. There are too many people who just want a handout. And sometimes, if a person can't work because they're sick, because they're taking care of someone who's sick, or something like that, then you might have to just give money. But if you can support a business, especially the business of a widow, then I think we should." Casey Hill added his opinion.

"What do you say, Pastor?" Millie Sanderson turned to him with her brows raised.

"I think she's part of our community. I think her candles are excellent quality. I've heard multiple people say that not only do they burn for a long time and give off a beautiful scent, but they add warmth and cheer to the church in January. An added bonus is that we would be supporting a widow, as the Bible commands, and also a member of our congregation and our community. I say we purchase the candles."

He wasn't going to add that last part, because he was new, and he didn't want to be rocking the boat or commanding everyone. Except... he was the pastor. He was supposed to be the leader. The shepherd, too, of course, but also the leader of the church. As he had been reminded several times this evening, that's what they hired him for. Not just his preaching, not just to visit people, but to lead the church in the direction it should go, following Jesus. He couldn't help but think that Jesus would probably buy Olivia's candles.

"All right then. If that's what the pastor thinks, I'll fall in line behind him." Bob Knapp nodded his head and crossed his arms over his chest, stretching his legs out and crossing his ankles.

It wasn't exactly a submissive pose, but his tone was conciliatory, and Mark nodded. "I appreciate your support. I was thinking to myself that if Jesus were here, I'm pretty sure he would buy Olivia's candles, not just because they're great candles, but because she's a member of the church and a widow." He paused. "He would probably even help her make them."

A small murmur of laughter rippled around the circle, while everyone nodded in agreement.

"Well, Pastor, I guess since you're the one that's supposed to be the most like Jesus, you should go offer to help."

They all laughed, but as the meeting went on and Noah came in, slipping in in time to talk about the music at the Christmas Eve service, Mark tucked that idea in the back of his head. He probably should offer to help her. Not just because he was a pastor, but as the Secret Saint, they hadn't been able to find a whole lot of things that they could do to give Olivia a hand. She was very tight-lipped about her needs, and Noah said the few times that they had tried to give her an envelope of cash, he'd seen she had passed it on to someone who was even more desperately in need than she was.

But helping her make them and purchasing her candles were two things that he could do.

He did not stop to think that perhaps there were ulterior motives. After all, he was the pastor, and he wasn't supposed to have any of those.

Chapter Seven

"Ibelieve that's everything. Meeting adjourned," Mark said, folding the paper he held in his hands in two and standing up from his chair.

"Pastor, if it's okay with you, I'd like to convene an emergency meeting for the town emergency management committee. Because of the weather," Ben Tucker said, standing up from his chair and speaking in a low tone to the pastor. His words were quick, like he was afraid that people would leave before he was able to do that.

"Totally fine with me."

"Thanks," Ben said. Then he looked around at the people still mostly sitting in their chairs. "If everyone who is on the town emergency management committee would please stay, I'd like to have a word with you all. The weather doesn't look good."

"I heard we're supposed to get a good bit of snow," Mark said, wondering if there would even be services for the first Christmas that he was here at his new church.

"The latest weather models I've seen have doubled the original estimates. You hardly ever see the forecasted amount go up. Usually they adjust down."

"Yeah, they start out scaring everyone to death, and then we barely ever get anything," Mark said. And then it sunk in. "Double? I heard one to two feet."

"Yeah. They're forecasting up to three feet now."

"Wow. I don't think I've ever been in a storm that dumped three feet of snow. Not here in Virginia."

"Sometimes in the mountains we can get a good bit. I think you came from a lower elevation."

"I did. And I've heard about road closures and that type of thing up here, but three feet of snow?" He could hardly believe it.

And at Christmas.

Lord? Isn't it important that we celebrate the birth of your son? Why would you schedule a snowstorm at this time of year? How about January?

As soon as he thought those things, he apologized to the Lord right away.

You know best, God. I'm sorry. I don't know anything. But your master plan is perfect, whatever it is. He paused, and then he added, *But, God? Snow? At Christmas? Three feet?*

Maybe he wasn't qualified to be a pastor. Maybe his faith wasn't strong enough. Maybe he should get a job where not so much of him was required.

It wasn't the first time he didn't feel qualified to do the job that he knew God had called him to do. In fact, most of the time he didn't feel qualified.

People had gathered back around, sitting back down, and a few more people walked in the door.

Mark could see Ben texting on his phone, asking people to show up quickly.

"You probably ought to stop in at Olivia's and let her know that she has the order for the church. I know in past years, it's taken her a really long time to fulfill it, since it's such a large order. Especially this time of year. Pastor Johnson always tried to get the order done early in the fall."

"I know. I wish we could've been on this sooner, but I wasn't voted in until earlier this month."

"I know. And Pastor Johnson said he didn't want to lock you into anything that you didn't want to do. Plus, I think Pastor Johnson's mind was more on his son and visiting him than it was on leaving the church in order." Mrs. Tucker shook her head, her lips pressed together.

"I think the man was right. His duty is to his family first, right after God. As important as it is for a pastor to shepherd the flock, he has to shepherd his family and put them in the correct position in his life."

He had been told that over and over again as he had prepared for the ministry. That ministry could be all-consuming, because there were always people with needs. But God gave him a family, and he didn't want to lose his family while he was busy taking care of his flock.

Of course, God hadn't seen fit to bless him with a family yet.

Maybe it was because God didn't think he could handle both a church and a wife and children.

"Okay, I think everyone's here. If we could all settle down and get started, this shouldn't take very long." Ben glanced around the room, and his eyes landed on Mark. "Pastor, if you want to stay, you're welcome."

"I don't mind listening in. But now that I have the floor, I did want to offer the church as a sanctuary or potential emergency shelter."

"That's great. That was actually one of the things I needed to talk to everyone about. Are you sure?"

"There's plenty of room, and I can check the storage shed out back. I'm pretty sure there were some extra sleeping bags in there that Pastor Johnson said they used one time to send kids to camp."

"I think you might be right about that."

"There were twenty of them, and as far as I know they're still there," Mrs. Tucker volunteered.

"All right then. We'll keep that in mind."

Mark listened as Ben ran the meeting, talking about the potential for large amounts of snow and how anything over two and a half feet was going to shut roads down for several days at the very least, and probably more like a week, until the plow trucks were able to get everyone plowed out.

He still couldn't believe that the Lord would be doing that this close to Christmas. But he knew any doubt wondering whether or not this was the best thing for the church showed his lack of faith. Rather than questioning God at the timing of the storm, he needed to learn to say, *Lord, show me what you want me to learn out of this. It seems like a crazy thing to have happen, but I know you're in charge. You can calm the storm anytime you want to, or you can whip one up as well. It's all in your hands. And I'm going to assume it's for my good and your glory. So if there's something I need to do, something I need to learn, someone I need to talk to even, just show me, Lord. Help me to surrender to whatever you have for me.*

He felt better after he said that. More confident. After all, he believed all of those words. God was totally in control, and there was no reason for him to be anything but absolutely sure that God would have his best interest at heart.

The meeting was short and quick, with everyone having a job or two to do to make sure that everyone in town would be okay, even if the electricity went out and the roads were not cleared.

Someone was bringing in a supply of milk and bread from a grocery store down at the bottom of the mountain. After all, whether or not they needed it, they couldn't survive a storm without it. At least, that was the joke going around. Still, milk would stay fresh if they had three feet of snow, even if the electricity went out, since they could just stick it in the snow to stay cold.

As the meeting adjourned, Mark walked out, talking to Mrs. Tucker and Bob Knapp, who had volunteered to go down the mountain and get the load of groceries.

"I better get out of here before the snow starts. I'm pretty sure the first snowflakes should start falling late tonight."

"You can be back in plenty of time if you leave now. And the grocery stores are open until nine o'clock down there." Mrs. Tucker seemed to be shooing him out. And then, to Mark's surprise, she turned to him. "You probably oughta take a walk up and down Main Street and just make sure that people are prepared. Especially widows and anyone who might need your help."

When she said widows, Mark automatically thought of older women who might need their walk shoveled and to be reminded that they had a place to go in the church if they lost electricity and couldn't heat their house.

And then he remembered about Olivia.

He lifted his eyes to the candle shop and saw that there were still lights on in the back, although there was clearly a closed sign hanging on the front door.

"I'll do that," he said to Mrs. Tucker, who probably saw exactly where his eyes went, because she had a satisfied smile on her face.

She was matchmaking, was she?

Mark doubted it, but if she was, she was barking up the wrong tree. God was going to arrange his marriage, not Mrs. Tucker.

He said good night to Mrs. Tucker and took two steps before he realized that he was being an idiot. God was just as likely to use Mrs. Tucker to matchmake as he was to do it Himself in a divine manner. After all, God used humans, as sinful and imperfect as they were, to accomplish His will on earth. Why did Mark think that he would be any different? And what did he think was going to happen, anyway? An angel was going to come and drop the right woman in his lap?

He supposed he didn't really know. But he also supposed that it was like sanctification, or holiness even. God would do everything, but God also expected a person to do everything they could as well. It was an equal partnership, although without God, it was nothing.

With that thought, Mark tucked a scarf around his neck, settled his hat more firmly on his head, and walked out of the basement of the church. He would make sure everything was locked up later, but for now, he needed to go let Olivia know that she had a big order of candles to make, and also that the church was open if she needed it at any time during the storm.

He wasn't sure why his heart started to beat faster and something like anticipation tangled through his chest. But whatever it was, he ignored it. He had business as a pastor to take care of.

Chapter Eight

Olivia glanced out the window, worry drawing her brows down.

It was a sin to worry, she knew that, but how was she supposed to not worry? It was supposed to storm, and the last time it stormed, her lights were out for three days. Pastor Johnson had opened the church and allowed them to come stay, but she had no idea if the new pastor would do that or not. Plus, she had this last big rush order to do, and she didn't want to drop the ball on it, since unless the church came through with a last-minute order, it was her last big order before Christmas, and she did not want to risk not being able to fulfill it.

There were no snow flurries coming down yet, but that didn't mean that it couldn't start at any time.

She had checked her phone a half an hour prior, and in big red letters at the top of her weather app, it had said that the storm was intensifying faster than predicted and was shaping up to be the worst storm of the century.

They often liked to scare people with wording like that, while whatever weather event they were talking about turned out to be a nothing burger, but just about the time she didn't listen, they would actually be right for a change.

"Are you almost done, Mommy?" Aiden asked from over in the corner where her boys played.

"I'm really not. It's going to be at least another hour, maybe two. Aren't you guys happy over there? You have your favorite trucks."

"I'm hungry," Aiden said, his lip coming out just ever so slightly.

"Well, I might have something that will help with that," Olivia said, having anticipated this very thing.

Thankfully, both of her boys loved fruit, and she had a container of blueberries in the small refrigerator under the counter, where she also kept juice and yogurt.

"How would you guys like to eat some blueberries?"

"I love blueberries!" Aiden exclaimed, jumping up and leading his twin over where they took the blueberries from her hands, thanking her before they went back over and sat down with the open container between them.

They would munch on the berries and probably eat the entire thing.

She gave them an indulgent smile. A knock on the door startled her.

She squinted, trying to see if she recognized whoever it was standing on the other side. It couldn't be a customer, because she could see that she had flipped the sign. Sometimes she forgot, but everyone in town knew that when the lights in the shop were off, it meant she was closed, whether she'd remembered about the sign or not.

Was that the new preacher?

"You guys be good, okay?"

"We're being good!" Aiden said, grinning.

She didn't tell them that she meant they were supposed to continue to be good. Instead, she went around the counter and walked toward the door.

The church meeting was tonight, and maybe Pastor Mark was

here to let her know whether or not she got the candle order. It was cutting it close, and she half expected that the church would've said that they didn't want to spend the money at this late date.

Steeling herself for whatever news he had, she turned the lock and opened the door.

"Pastor. Come on in."

"Miss Olivia. Thank you."

"You don't have to call me Miss Olivia." She laughed, shaking her head as she shut the door.

"It's just a respect thing. But I won't if it makes you uncomfortable."

"I kind of feel like you might be younger than I am, so it feels odd."

"I think we're probably about the same age," Pastor Mark said, and then he looked away, as though he realized that was a personal topic and he felt like he shouldn't be discussing it.

"I assume you came for more than to talk about how old you are. Do you mind if I work while we chat?" she asked, going back over to the counter where she had been putting labels on the batch of candles that was cool.

"Is there something I can help you with?" he asked, as though he had all of the time in the world.

"I was putting labels on this batch, and if you do that, then I can go over here and add the last ingredients to this wax and start dipping."

"Show me how, and I'm happy to help."

She gave him a look, and then shrugged. "All right."

She walked behind the counter, and he followed.

"Hey there, boys. Looks like you're eating blueberries. That's my favorite."

"Our favorite too!" Aidan said.

"But we'll share," Ethan said. It was funny how kids could come up with something that just made her feel like the proudest mom in the entire world. Her kid offered to share his favorite snack.

It looked a little bit like Aiden was trying to shush Ethan and give him a hard time for saying that, but hey, at least one of her boys was starting to learn some of the things that she had been teaching.

"I'm not hungry tonight, but thanks," Pastor Mark said, sounding totally at ease with her kids. She'd seen adults who seemed to melt into a muddled mess when they saw children, like somehow little kids scared them. Pastor Mark was not one of those people.

"You're pretty good with kids," she said casually as she picked up the labels that she'd printed on the computer.

"They seem to like me. I'm not sure why. I don't have any of my own."

"You're not married," she said casually, not digging for information, but she would've been surprised had he had any children, considering that he had no wife.

"That's true. No wife, no kids."

"But you have a mom," Aiden said, having gotten up and wandered over to see the newcomer.

"I used to. That's true. But she's in heaven now, along with my dad."

Olivia didn't say anything. He was kind of young to have lost both parents. She could relate a little, since she hadn't talked to her parents since they'd given her a hard time about marrying her husband.

"Do you have a twin?" Aiden asked, after Olivia had shown Pastor Mark how to put the labels on the jars.

It wasn't too uncommon for townspeople to help each other out, but... it felt a little weird that the pastor was in here. She wanted to ask how the meeting went. Maybe him coming in and offering to help was an attempt to soften the blow that she wasn't going to get the candle order today.

"Nope. No twin, no siblings."

"You're all alone in the world?" she asked, feeling like she could relate. Although her parents weren't dead. They just weren't talking to her.

"My church family has always been my family. I guess I just don't know it any other way. Maybe the idea that I don't have siblings and my parents are gone has helped me to stick closer to my church family. God has a way of working those things out."

"I guess I feel closer to the people in the town."

"Your parents are dead too?"

"No." She didn't say anything more. She didn't want to explain that there was a rift between them. She knew in Christian circles that it was kind of frowned on for a person not to be getting along with her family. After all, the Bible clearly said that if you don't love your brother whom you can see, how can you love God whom you can't?

She found it was a lot easier to love God than her brother, though. Or her mother. As the case may be.

"These are pretty. Did you design them?" Pastor Mark said as he put one on and held it up for her inspection.

"That's perfect. And yes, I did. I enjoy doing that kind of creative stuff. Especially after I've spent a lot of time working with my hands."

"I would think coming up with new recipes for candles would exercise your creative abilities."

"Definitely. I love that side of the business. But there are times where I'm just doing one after the other after the other and it takes no creativity at all, just a willingness to buckle in and do the work."

"That's what a lot of life is. A willingness to buckle in and do the work. Adult life anyway."

She grinned, looking over at the boys playing in the corner, popping blueberries into their mouths as they made truck noises and crawled on their hands and knees, one hand on their trucks, pushing them in a circle that must have been a racetrack or something.

"Yeah. The good old days, right?"

He looked at the boys and then shook his head. "I had a great childhood, but I love what I do, and I have no desire to go back there."

"Sometimes I wish I could go back permanently. The days where

I had no pressure, no worry about whether or not I was going to be able to buy groceries. No questions about whether or not my business was going to be able to stay solvent and pay for our health insurance."

"That's rough. But I have good news, I hope."

"Really?" she asked, her heart stuttering. She couldn't help stopping what she was doing and looking at him expectantly.

"Yeah. The church voted tonight to go ahead with their normal order of candles. But I know it's late. Pastor Johnson said he usually ordered them in September."

"Oh. Thank you, Jesus," she said, closing her eyes. Then she opened them and spoke immediately. "It doesn't matter how late it is. I will get the order done. I... I needed this order. But I didn't want to say how badly, because I didn't want the church to order it out of pity."

"That's not what happened. I think people really appreciate the quality of your candles, the delicate scent that does not overwhelm but lasts through the entire burning of the candle, but especially the way they brighten the church up in the dark month of January."

"That's awesome. It makes it even better that you're helping me tonight, because I definitely need to get these done if I'm going to have any prayer at all of getting the church candles done, especially if we lose electricity for a day or two with the storm."

"I've heard that's a real possibility," he said as he stuck another label on and carefully set the candle down with the other ones he had finished.

He was not taking things too fast, but he wasn't slow either. He was a good worker.

"The last I heard is that it's going to be more intense than they anticipated. It's up to three feet of snow. The last time we got two feet, I didn't have electricity for two days, and Pastor Johnson let me stay in the church."

"That reminds me. We're opening up the church as an emergency shelter, so if you lose electricity, come on over. There's a generator, and we even have sleeping bags, apparently."

"Well, we have plenty of sleeping bags, and we'll be over then if we lose electricity, because we don't have a generator, and I don't want the boys to freeze."

"I'll make sure that they don't. And there's plenty of toys in the nursery."

"They'll be thrilled to be able to play with the nursery toys again. They graduated from nursery when they turned three, and they've been sad ever since."

Chapter Nine

ark pulled the last sleeping bag out of the dryer.

His washer had been doing laundry nonstop for what felt like forever. But all the sleeping bags the church had were now fully washed and dried and ready for the storm.

He wasn't entirely sure that people would actually come to the church, but he wanted to be prepared. About the time he wasn't, the lights would be out for a week.

He thought about Olivia in the candle shop by herself with her twins. She hadn't mentioned not having a good relationship with her parents, nor had she mentioned any siblings. He wished he would've asked, because he wondered now if she was truly alone. As alone as he was. Although he didn't really think of himself as being alone, not with his church family. But not everyone was as involved in the church as he was, of course, considering that he was the pastor.

Still, there was a nagging sense of needing to make sure that Olivia was okay. He wasn't entirely sure that it was just because she was alone, either.

He felt an interest in her that went above and beyond his pastoral duties.

Lord, I don't want to be inappropriate or act out of place. If how I feel about Olivia is going to cause me to stumble, I pray that you'll show me somehow that I need to change things so that your work is never in jeopardy.

That was one thing about being a pastor. Other people had a tendency to hold him to a higher standard than what any normal person was held to.

He already held himself to a high standard, but with the added pressure of other people, sometimes it got to be a little much.

That's when he would go to the Lord and admit that he cared a lot about what other people thought, but it was mostly because he didn't want to drive people away from the Lord because of his actions.

The single biggest reason that people gave him for not going to church was because it was full of hypocrites.

He couldn't always square that, because no one was perfect. Every single person who came to church was a sinner, no matter how long they had been a Christian, up to and including the man behind the pulpit. He ought to know.

But still, people acted all holier-than-thou at times within the church walls, and then after they left, it was shocking to him how Christians could act worse than non-Christians.

He shook his head. Those were all thoughts of a pastor, and problems that he couldn't solve. Yes, there were hypocrites in the church. There always had been, and they always would be, because humans were sinful creatures. And they were just as prone to being hypocrites as they were to being liars and adulterers and thieves and fornicators. Unfortunately.

But of course, that didn't mean that it wasn't his job to preach on all of those things from the pulpit, as well as to remind everyone that no matter how much they sinned, God still loved them. It was the message of hope and grace that he loved the most, but sin still needed to be preached on as well.

His next sermon was practically writing itself, he thought to himself as he finished folding up the sleeping bag and carried it through the room that connected the parsonage to the church. It was clever the way whoever had designed it, where a person could walk from the church to the parsonage without ever setting foot outside.

He put his hands on his hips and looked around the big activity room. Most of the tables were down, although there were a few up in the corner where people could eat if it came to that. There were plenty of spaces for families to stake out an area for their own. He even had a few tents, cots and camp chairs as well.

Lord, I don't want anyone to get hurt in the storm, but I am thankful that we have a place for people to go. Please let people be willing to come and be safe here. Help me to be a blessing to them.

Curious to see if the snow had started, Mark walked to the window to look out on the road, as headlights flashed and a car pulled into the parking lot of the church. It didn't seem like it was going very fast, and he couldn't tell exactly what was wrong with it, but it didn't look quite right. Maybe it was lopsided in some way. He squinted to get a better look, noting that there were a few flurries coming down, but nothing major had started, at least not yet.

Maybe his eyes were deceiving him, and there was nothing wrong with the car. Maybe someone was stopping by the church to deliver some supplies.

Or it could just be someone meeting someone else. Regardless, he turned around, walking back into the parsonage where he could grab his coat, purposefully shoving his arms into it and opening up the door and hurrying out.

Whoever it was had already gotten out of their car and was looking at the front wheel.

It looked like a woman, although they had a hat and coat on, and in the dark, with only the streetlights for light, he couldn't tell for sure.

Still, he was pretty sure it was someone who needed help.

"Excuse me?" he said as he came around the front of the car, not wanting to startle whoever it was.

The person looked up, her eyes wide, and immediately he recognized Olivia.

"Olivia," he said, thinking it interesting that he had just been thinking about her. He glanced at the wheel in front of her. "A flat tire?" It was a question, but a statement as well, because it was obvious the tire was flat.

"Yeah. And I know I don't have a spare, because I didn't replace it when the other front tire went flat earlier this fall. I had intended to put snow tires on closer to winter, and I guess I was hoping they would hold out a bit longer."

"I've done that before. You always hope there's a little more life in them." That, and he always hoped that he would somehow have more money in the next month than he did in the current one. But he didn't say that. If that was what Olivia was doing, he didn't want to embarrass her by pointing it out.

"Exactly."

"Do you have the boys with you?" he asked, as a gust of wind blew and he shoved his hands deep into the pockets of his coat, while a long strand of Olivia's hair blew across her face.

She pushed it back with one mittened hand and glanced at the car.

"Yeah. I just got finished delivering the candles that needed to go before the storm, and I have one more delivery to make, although... it doesn't have to go."

"How about you guys come on into the parsonage and get warmed up, while I call Tom's Towing and see if he'd be able to come out and put a tire on. I think I can figure out what size these are."

Relief washed over her face, but only for a second. Then her brows drew down in a stubborn, mulish look.

"I couldn't possibly impose."

"You're not imposing at all. And I don't mind or I wouldn't have offered."

"It's not that far." She bit her lip. "But I didn't put coats on the boys. I just assumed... they're only wearing their jammies, because it was so close to bedtime."

"And my house is right here." Then he realized that sometimes it was better to sweeten the pot a bit, so to speak. "I've been getting the church rec room ready just in case the electricity goes out in town and people need a place to shelter. Would you mind coming in, checking it out and giving me any advice or tips that you have?"

Yeah. That did it. She tilted her head, and then a smile lifted the corners of her mouth up. "Sure. I'd be happy to."

"All right. I'll give you a hand getting the boys in, and then you can look it over while I call Tom's."

"Are you sure you don't mind?" she asked, brows knit together.

"I told you. I don't mind at all. I visited Tom earlier this week, and I'm actually welcoming a chance to reach out and to remind him that the invitation to come to church is still open." He winked at her, and she laughed.

The sound made his insides twirl a bit. Why was the sound of her laughter so intriguing?

He walked around the car to the other side and opened the door.

"What are you doing?" Aiden asked, staring up at him from his booster seat.

"Your mom and I are gonna get you out of your booster seat and take you inside for a bit. She's gonna check things out and let me know how I did getting ready for the storm that's coming."

"Mommy was making deliveries before the storm. And we almost had them all done," Aidan said, obviously parroting something that Olivia had said.

"Is it snowing yet?" Ethan asked his mother as she unbuckled him.

Mark looked up, and his eyes met Olivia's across the backseat. He smiled at her, and while there still seemed to be some worry on her face, she smiled back. "Not yet. And we're gonna go check and see if the church is ready for it to snow."

Aiden came to him easily, his outgoing and inquisitive personality clearly on display.

Ethan clung a little tighter to his mother, but he didn't seem overly fearful. Probably as long as his twin was around, he would be okay.

The parsonage door was closer, so Mark walked up the walk, and then opened it, holding it for Olivia to go through first.

"Thank you," she murmured as she walked in.

"Head to the left. There's a door there, and that leads through my office directly to the church."

"That's neat," Olivia said. "I've been in the parsonage, and I've been in the church, but I've never used the secret passageway," she said.

He laughed. He hadn't really thought about it as a secret passageway, but he supposed it probably was something that was designed for only the pastor to use. Especially since it went through a room that he used for his office, and he suspected Pastor Johnson had too, since there were empty bookshelves in there when he moved in.

"It's just through that door right there," he said, flipping on the lights as he walked in after her. "And don't mind the mess. I don't have things quite unpacked."

"That doesn't surprise me. It seemed like it was more important to you to get to know the people of your congregation rather than getting everything in line perfectly."

She was making a general statement, he was pretty sure, although he also thought that she seemed a little impressed.

He kind of hoped so. He'd always thought that people were more important than things. And his ministry was more about people than anything else. Even more important than giving a good sermon. Although that was the second thing that he spent the most time on during the week for his job. Although spending time in personal prayer and Bible study was probably his top priority. How could he help others if he wasn't nurturing his own relationship with the Lord?

"So this is where this door goes. I've always wondered about it," Olivia said.

"It's pretty nice. You can get to the parsonage without getting wet on rainy days or cold on winter ones."

"Yeah, I like the way it's set up," Olivia said, stopping to look around.

Ethan wiggled a little in her arms, and she set him down, his footed pajama bottoms making a soft swishing sound on the floor.

"The boys won't hurt anything. In fact, if we have people coming, there'll be lots of little kids running around hopefully, so they can play if they want."

"All right. Thanks for letting me know."

"I'll be back in a minute. I want to double-check the size on those tires and give Tom a call."

"All right. Thanks," Olivia said, although from the set of her shoulders and the way she pulled her lip in between her teeth, he suspected she wasn't very comfortable.

Hopefully, he could come back in and put her at ease.

Chapter Ten

Olivia looked around the activity room. There was a corner with tables and chairs set up, where she assumed people were welcome to sit and eat. Boxes of paper plates and plastic silverware sat underneath the table. Sleeping bags were stacked in one corner, and there were several cases of bottled water along one wall.

As she investigated further, she saw totes full of snacks, and more totes full of toys that ranged from toddler age to board games that entire families could enjoy.

There were blankets that smelled like they'd been freshly washed, and she also saw several tents and camp chairs stacked against the far wall.

She couldn't imagine anyone needing anything else, although on a hunch, she walked into the kitchen and opened up the refrigerator.

As she had suspected, there were gallons of milk, along with bags full of vegetables and fruit.

It seemed like Pastor Mark had thought of everything.

When had he had time to do all of this in addition to all the other things he was doing?

He certainly was taking his job of pastoring his flock seriously.

Okay, Lord, I thought that getting a flat tire was the absolute worst thing that could ever happen to me, but I have to admit coming in here and seeing how prepared Pastor Mark is for the people who might need a place to stay during the storm has been eye-opening. Obviously the man is dedicated to his job, and truly cares about the people. I'm also really impressed at his foresight, and the thoughtful things that he stocked in order to make being away from their home as pleasant an experience as possible.

On a hunch, she walked to the restroom and saw that it too was well stocked with extra bathroom tissue, as well as paper towels and soap.

She smiled a little when she noticed that there were no extra feminine products. Pastor Mark probably hadn't thought of such a thing, but she supposed that she might be able to raid her own bathroom closet and cover that deficiency without mentioning anything to Pastor Mark.

As she walked out of the restroom, she saw Mark coming in the door, his eyes sweeping over the room, lingering for a moment on her boys, who were playing with a couple of the toys from the totes, until they continued on until he found her over against the far wall.

"I'm here," she said, thinking that he was acting a little bit like he was afraid that she was going to skip town after he had left her alone for three minutes.

No, that wasn't fair. He just wanted to make sure that she was okay. Obviously, the man had a spiritual gift of helping. Or he just truly was concerned about people. She couldn't fault him for that. Especially when his job almost demanded it.

"What do you think?" he asked as he started across the large room.

She started walking to meet him, and they stood in the middle of the room, side by side, naturally turning to where her boys played in the corner.

"I'm impressed. I have to admit it."

"Really?"

"Truly. I think you've thought of everything."

"I had a little bit of help. I called Mrs. Tucker and asked what Pastor Johnson had done when they used the church several years ago for an emergency shelter."

"I bet her insights were invaluable."

"They were. They had just put the generator in, according to her, because that winter was the worst on record, and the first snowstorm put power out for three days, and the church wasn't able to help out much, since there was no power here either."

"I have to admit, putting a generator in was a really wise decision. That's pretty expensive for a normal family to be able to afford. I know I don't have one."

"I've never priced them, but I do know I've never lived in a house that had one."

"I priced them out several years ago when we lost electricity. And yeah, it was way too much. But... it feels a little bit like charity coming here too. You know?"

She didn't want to admit that much. She definitely didn't want to put a damper on what he was doing. She wanted to encourage him. She just didn't want to be the kind of person who needed handouts from anyone, including the church in a snowstorm. Although... she knew that it was a perfectly normal thing.

"There's no shame in needing help once in a while," Mark said, as though he could read her mind.

She nodded, and then pointed at the sleeping bags. "Are those the ones they bought for camp a couple of years ago?" She wanted to change the subject, because she didn't want to think about all the things that she owed everyone who had ever helped her. She wanted to be able to stand on her own two feet. To provide for her family herself, without depending on anyone else.

But was that really the way God intended it?

"They sure are. And while I'm thinking about it, Tom said he'd be right over. He's gearing up, figuring that he'll be busy during the storm, and he wanted to get that tire changed before the snow started coming down."

"Thank you. I appreciate you making the call."

"I had ulterior motives. I told you. I reminded him that the church is open on Sunday, whether there's electricity or not. I happen to know someone who is rather good at making candles, and I think I might be able to pull a few strings in case we need extra."

"Are you serious?" she asked, laughing.

"I sure am. I don't see any reason why we can't use the candles that we ordered for the Christmas Eve service, if you have any of those ready."

"I actually have a few that were left over from last year. I was going to include those in the order this year. I always make a few extra, just in case some don't turn out." She lifted a shoulder. "I also have some candles set back in my storage room. The ones where the label was crooked, or the wick wasn't centered properly, or I even have a few that didn't smell quite the way I was expecting, and I haven't quite decided how to label them. I mean, 'chicken poop' is not exactly a selling point."

"No. How bad do they smell? Maybe we don't want to use those in an enclosed area where people can't escape for possibly days."

"True. They smell pretty awful. Not everything I try is a success." Boy, wasn't that the truth. She figured she'd probably failed more than she'd succeeded. But wasn't that true for everyone?

"I have a bunch of candles that I've been experimenting with, some more successful than others, but you're welcome to as many of those as you'd like."

"What do you usually do with them?"

"Sometimes I give them away as gifts. Sometimes I end up selling them if I deem them successful, and I'll include them in a variety pack, or as a special at the counter, but they always go for less than I normally charge, just because I never have a whole bunch of them."

"I see. Well, I'm pretty sure I can get the church to pay for it. After all, if we're going to be a shelter for people, we should be able to provide light at the very least."

"You don't have to do that. I'll donate them. I should've offered to begin with. I was thinking about all the things that you have ready, and how organized and thoughtful you are, and I never even thought about candles for light."

"We can argue about what I owe you later, but I'll take whatever you're willing to give."

"All right. Once Tom has my tire fixed, I'll grab a couple of boxes and drive them back over."

Just then lights flashed in the window, and she turned toward them.

"I think Tom's here."

"That was quick. I'm impressed."

She shifted uneasily, feeling a little bit like she was imposing.

"If you were doing something and you need to keep working, don't let me get in your way."

"Not at all. I wasn't doing anything important. I just finished washing the last of the sleeping bags. But don't forget, part of my job is talking to the people in town and getting to know them. So technically, I'm on the clock right now."

He made it seem like it was no problem at all for him to be standing there talking to her. But if she were in charge of the church, and she was expecting a whole pile of people to be coming to shelter there, she would be running around like a chicken with her head cut off.

"Are you sure there isn't anything you need to do yet?"

He waved an arm around the building. "Do you see anything that needs to be done?"

"No. Other than picking up the toys that my boys have gotten out. I did caution them to only play with a few things."

"I figure about two seconds after the first kid gets here, the toys will be out and a mess from then until everyone leaves and someone picks them up. That's just kind of the nature of children, isn't it?"

"How do you know so much about kids when you don't have any of your own?"

"Maybe someday I will. I feel like God has a family for me somewhere, but... it hasn't happened yet."

"So you want to get married?" She didn't know why she was asking that. What did it matter to her? But she found herself unusually interested and hanging on his answer.

"Yes. I feel like a pastor is more effective when he has a wife beside him. Someone who can help him. And not to be sexist, but..."

"That's not sexist. The Bible clearly says that the woman was created to be the man's helpmeet. Which I always understood to be a helper that's fit for him. So it's up to the woman to shape herself and adjust herself to be a helper in whatever her man does."

She couldn't help the sadness that had entered her voice. That's what she had always believed. She had helped Cam however she could. Of course, being that he was in the military, it wasn't like he had his own business that she was helping him with, but she tried to make their home a haven, to make sure that whatever he was facing with his job or his deployment, talking to her was an oasis of peace and love and laughter. She felt like that was the best way she could help him.

"I feel like there was more that you didn't say," Pastor Mark finally said after a long pause.

"I guess sometimes I just wonder what God was thinking, you know?"

"I certainly have those thoughts myself. But the Bible says that His ways are higher than ours. So I have to accept that. What causes you to wonder?"

"It's true that his ways are higher than ours. Sometimes it's pretty amazing how He works things out. But... I didn't go to college or get any kind of training for a job, because I wanted to be a stay-at-home mom. I feel like that's part of what's wrong with our country today. So many women are more concerned about their careers and their hair and their nails and buying whatever it is that they feel like is going to make them happy, and they don't focus on being a good wife, on making their house a home. On raising the children and doing all the things that a woman was created to do. And then, my husband died. And all of a sudden, I am left holding the bag, so to speak. Because I've got two little boys who are depending on me, and no career, no way of earning any income, no education or anything. It just... it seemed like I was doing what I know God wanted me to, and it bit me hard."

"Is the candle shop doing okay?"

"It's paying the bills."

"Then God provided."

She kept her mouth shut. He was right. God didn't provide the way she thought He should—with a husband who didn't die. But...

She sighed, the air seeming to come from the very depths of her soul. "I know you're right. We've never gotten hungry. We've never lacked for anything essential. But... I still just can't help but question why God would take my husband after I had tried so hard to do what I felt God wanted me to, and what God commands for women in the Bible."

"I guess I could see why you're questioning that. But I also see that God has provided bountifully for you. You didn't need any of those things that the world tells you you do. And when you lost your husband, God came through, showing that when you follow Him and do things His way, He doesn't leave you, but always takes care of you."

She had never thought about it like that. She had just questioned God allowing her husband to die. She hadn't thought about how He had, as Mark said, totally taken care of them. Even though she didn't have an education and wasn't planning on using her candles to support the family.

"But there are so many women who want to have a career. Who want to be outside of the home. Who don't want to stay home with their children, who don't want to be a wife and mother according to what the Bible tells us to do, and yet they have husbands. I guess I look around and don't understand."

"I've found that for me, personally, it's best for me to keep my eyes on Jesus and look at Him. Think about what He wants, think about what He's doing, think about how I can be more like Him, because when I start looking around at everyone else, I start to be very discontent."

Olivia snapped her mouth closed. How did he give her a mini sermon, convict her so thoroughly, and not make her feel bad, but make her realize that he was completely and totally right, all in the span of five minutes?

"You're very good at your job," she finally said. And she meant it.

But he looked confused. "What brought that on?" he asked, as though he hadn't just delivered a sermon in a casual conversation and not made her feel preached at, but rather like it was a subtle reminder and a big encouragement.

"Just that we're having a conversation, and all of a sudden, I realize that I've been listening to a sermon, but I didn't even realize it, because you made it so natural, so much a natural part of what we were talking about. I didn't feel like you were slamming me, or judging me, or finding me lacking. And I have to admit that a lot of times I do feel that way. Christians judge, you know?"

"They definitely do. I think sometimes Christians are the least Christlike people on the planet. Even non-Christians a lot of times are more Christlike than Christians are. But maybe that's why those people became Christians to begin with, because they knew they really needed the Lord."

"And I'm being judgmental by judging Christians. Aren't I?" She laughed a little and shook her head. "I hate it when I become what I hate, but it happens more often than I'd like to admit."

"To you too? Because I find that's true for me. It's almost like I dislike something because I know I am that thing, subconsciously if not consciously."

They laughed together, and then lapsed into silence. It was a comfortable silence, though, and Olivia didn't feel like she needed to scramble to find something to say. She felt like Mark, far from judging her, admired her. And enjoyed talking to her. There were just certain people that a person met who were capable of making someone feel like they mattered. Mark had that gift.

"I told Tom to come in when he was finished, and I'm pretty sure I just saw a figure walking up the sidewalk. I'm going to scoot through the office and go see."

"I can come with you. Although I left my purse in the car."

He waved a hand. "I'll deal with it. I might've just been seeing things."

She kind of thought he might be saying that so she wouldn't follow him. But she didn't want to push in when he specifically told her not to. Maybe he wanted her to watch her kids. She wasn't sure.

Regardless, she did not follow him out, but turned, looking around the room one more time, trying to think of anything he had missed. She saw a shelf of books, and even a broom, a dustpan, and a sweeper in the corner. Along with boxes of disinfectant wipes. And tissues.

Truly, she thought he'd thought of everything.

And then she thought about how comfortable it was to talk to him. And how impressed she was that he applied the Bible so casually yet competently to everyday life.

There was definitely a lot to admire in Mark Stevens.

Chapter Eleven

he rattling of the parsonage windows woke Mark from a restless sleep.

Gusts of wind so strong he braced himself for the windows to implode and shatter all over the floor rocked the house.

He went from being partially asleep to wide awake in an instant. Sitting up, he grabbed his phone, bringing up the weather app.

Red highlighted words swam before his eyes before they focused. *Storm gathering intensity, worse than forecasters feared.*

Yeah, he could see that. He hadn't expected this terrible wind. Sheltered as they were in the mountains, it seemed more like a blizzard than anything he could remember.

Throwing his feet over the side of the bed, he looked out to see snow whipping by, and the windows rattled again.

He reached over to turn his bedside light on so he could see to find his shoes, which he'd left beside the bed so he could find them easily in case he got up in the middle of the night, but when he snapped the light, nothing happened.

It took a moment to register. The electricity was out.

That sent a new spike of adrenaline through him, as he ran over in his mind the things that he needed to do. Go start the generator, make sure there was heat in the fellowship hall, then... see if the roads were clear enough for him to jump in his car and drive around to see if anyone needed him to pick them up and bring them to the church.

He glanced out the window, trying to see how much snow had fallen.

With the wind, it was hard to tell, but he could still see some bare spots in the church parking lot, so he guessed that it was less than a couple of inches. He would still be able to get around.

Using his phone as a flashlight, he found where he'd set his clothes in a pile and quickly got dressed.

There was a part of him that was excited—this was his first real test as pastor of the Mistletoe Meadows community. Part of him was scared. The townspeople were used to Pastor Johnson and the way he did things, and maybe Mark would not measure up. Part of him had his mind on all of his parishioners, but there was one that came to the forefront of his mind, and as he hurried out to start the generator and make sure the heat was working in the fellowship hall, Olivia and her twins took up most of his thoughts. He wouldn't be able to concentrate on helping everyone else until he was sure she was taken care of.

As soon as he made sure the fellowship hall was warming, he got in his car and drove directly to her place.

He could look over and see that the streetlights were out, and he was pretty sure that meant that Olivia did not have heat.

If she lived above the shop with her boys, it was probably getting pretty cold, although he had no way of knowing what time the lights had gone out.

There were elderly people in his congregation, and several who had no close relatives to check on them, and he knew he couldn't spend as much time as he wanted to with Olivia, but he justified stopping at her place first because if he could get her to go over to the fellowship hall, she could help all the people who showed up while he drove around to see if there was anyone else he could help.

That seemed very logical in his brain, but if he were being honest, he knew the main reason he went over there first was because it was where he wanted to be.

He wished he would've gotten her phone number earlier as he knocked on the door. Could she even hear him over the roaring of the wind? If her windows were rattling the way his were, she probably couldn't.

He waited for a bit, and then rapped as hard as he could again.

What was he going to do if she didn't answer? He was almost certain she had no electricity.

Just as he was getting ready to lift his hand to rap a third time, a ghostly figure shifted through the darkness, coming into focus just as the lock on the door clicked and opened partway.

"Olivia. I assume you don't have electricity?" he asked, his eyes roving over her face, more concerned than he wanted to admit. She looked like she was fine, though.

"Yeah. I just woke up about five minutes ago and realized it was all off. The storm's come in a lot harder than what they were calling for."

"Yeah. I think there were some late developments that caused it to be a lot stronger than forecasted. I haven't seen any snowfall totals, but I figured if I didn't have electricity, and your porch light was out, you probably didn't have any either."

"No. But I think we'll be okay for a while and—"

"I was hoping that you would go over to the fellowship hall and help get people settled as I bring them in."

She paused, and he held his breath. He knew she had an independent streak, and she wanted to prove that she was okay on her own, but he just wanted her somewhere where she was safe. That way he didn't have to worry about her as he worked to help other people.

But that was selfish in a way. It also showed that his feelings for her went a lot deeper than what he wanted to admit, and probably deeper than hers. Funny how an emergency like this could show a person what they really felt inside.

"All right. Maybe you can come in and give me a hand with the boys?"

"I sure can. I left my car running along the sidewalk, so we don't have far to carry them."

"Thanks. I bedded them down behind the store tonight, since I figured we would probably lose power. I wasn't sure whether I would be carrying them out or not, and it's easier to do that if you don't have to go down the steps."

"That was smart on your part," he said. It would be a lot easier to get the boys out from the back room than it would be from their apartment upstairs. Although, he had to admit he was a little curious to see what it looked like. Olivia was creative and artistic, and he bet she had it decorated beautifully.

Where did that thought come from? He never noticed how people had their house decorated. He didn't really care. His job was to be concerned about their spiritual welfare, and their physical welfare second. However they chose to decorate or not decorate their house had absolutely no bearing on whether or not he did his job or how he did it either.

"Here's Aiden," Olivia whispered as she knelt down, then stood up with a little boy in her arms.

"Mommy?" Aiden said sleepily.

"It's Pastor Mark. We're going over to the church rec room for a bit. Snuggle in so you don't get cold."

"Why is it so dark?" Aidan asked, sounding slightly less sleepy.

"Because the electricity is out. We'll be able to use some of your mom's candles now," he said, hoping that the idea of the electricity being out didn't scare him.

"Mommy has some special candles set back. She told me."

He lifted his brows and looked back over his shoulder at Olivia, who came behind him. He couldn't see her face and couldn't meet her eyes, but he wondered what in the world Aiden meant by Mommy's special candles.

"I was experimenting with some different shaped candles that would be a little safer to use in a group setting like we'll have at the church. I don't know if these are going to work, but my goal was that they would be less likely to start a fire if they got tipped over."

"Interesting," he said, meaning it. He had never even considered trying to make safer candles.

"As soon as I get Ethan in the car, I'll run back in. I have the box right there on the floor by the door."

"I can get it. You get in the car with the boys and try to keep them calm so they don't get upset."

She made a small sound, and he hoped that meant that she was agreeing to his suggestion. He didn't really ask her—he was commanding—he didn't want her out in the cold any more than she needed to be.

"I have a small bookbag packed with extra clothes for us sitting right beside the box."

"I'll grab that too."

She made another noise, and this time he was pretty sure it was agreement. He wanted to thank her for not arguing with him at this point, but instead, he opened the car door and waited for her to duck in, scooting over on the backseat with Ethan on her lap before he set Aiden down beside her and closed the door.

He had gotten a look at her face, which, while her cheeks were red, her eyes were clear and calm.

There wasn't anything to be afraid of. There was plenty of food, and the generator at the church would keep them warm. Still, he appreciated her calmness at what must surely be a high-stress time for her, with her two twins needing her, and having to leave her home. Especially so close to Christmas.

He hurried back in, finding the box and the packed bag just where she said.

As he left, he twisted the lock on the knob and pulled the door shut. He didn't have a key to turn the deadbolt, but the doorknob lock should be enough. The weather certainly was not conducive to anyone going around trying to steal anything from the stores and businesses on Main Street. But stranger things had happened.

He hurried out into the gusting wind and blowing snow, opening the trunk and putting the bag and box in there.

He was completely frozen by the time he opened the door and settled down in his seat.

Olivia had the heater blowing on high, and the car had been running long enough that it was blowing warm air.

"That feels good," he said.

"I figured it would. Thank you for going back in and getting those things. It's freezing out."

"I think that must be why the wind is blowing so much. The temperature must've dropped thirty degrees since I went to bed, and that's only been a few hours."

"I think you're right. And the blowing snow doesn't help."

"No, it feels like ice shards cutting into my face."

He pulled out into the street, doing a U-turn and heading back to the church. The streets were deserted, with every business completely dark and no streetlights on. It almost looked like an alien landscape, dark, wind-swept, and cold.

"I'm gonna park as close to the door as I can. I can carry the boys in."

"I can get one of them. I think they're both awake anyway."

"I'm sorry. But I figured it was going to be pretty cold by morning. Especially with that wind."

"I'm glad you insisted. I really didn't want to come, and I was hoping that the lights would be back on and I wouldn't have to. There's just... I always feel like I need to do everything myself to prove that I can."

He glanced in the rearview mirror, meeting her eyes.

"But that's why I'm here. To help. And you letting me makes me feel like I'm doing my job."

"I'm glad it makes you feel good," she said, but there was still a note of sadness in her voice, like she wished that she was able to handle it.

"If your husband hadn't been killed, the two of you could do it together. But it's really difficult to be a single mom and do all the things that two people are supposed to do."

"You're a single person."

"I don't have children."

"That's true."

"He could be our dad," Aiden said, sounding hopeful and helpful at the same time.

Mark just about choked on his spit. Somewhere in the back of his head that thought had been going around. But Olivia had her own business, and he had promised God that he would marry a woman who would be able to help him with the work that he had to do. It wouldn't be fair to the people who hired him for him to bring a wife in that wasn't committed to working in the ministry as well. His job was the kind of job that both of them needed to be one hundred percent involved in.

"I'm sorry. They never knew their real dad. I talk about him all the time, but he's just pictures and stories. No memories."

Her voice came softly from the backseat as he pulled up to the door, wishing their conversation could continue. He was curious about her husband, and she hadn't mentioned anything in any of the other conversations that they'd had. But maybe once everyone was in and settled, and he was sure that he had done everything he could for the people of his congregation and the town of Mistletoe Meadows, maybe then they'd have some time to talk. He almost snorted. They would probably have time, but there would be no privacy.

He opened the door, hopped out, and then got Aiden from the backseat, still wrapped in a blanket, and carried him a few steps to the door. The fellowship hall was lit, a welcoming beacon amidst the darkness of the town as the generator rumbled in the background and the wind whipped around them.

"I'm gonna run back out and help your mom," he said as he set Aiden down.

Aiden gripped the blanket close and nodded, but for once didn't say anything.

Olivia had not worked her way out of the backseat with Ethan on her lap, and he was able to reach down and grab Ethan.

"Thanks. I'll grab the stuff in the back."

He nodded his head, because he figured arguing with her was pointless. But she could've come in and he would've gotten it gladly.

He figured she probably knew that, but what she said about wanting to be able to do things herself echoed in his mind. That wasn't necessarily biblical. Of course God wanted people to do their very best, but he also wanted people to allow others to help when they needed it. After all, if everyone was doing everything for themselves, there would be no need for anyone to help anyone. And sometimes when a person helped people, it grew on them. Of course, sometimes when they accepted help, it grew them as well. Maybe even more, especially for someone who was used to being able to do everything themselves.

But that was a lesson he could learn as well, because he liked to be the one taking care of others, not the one who had to be taken care of. So he could definitely understand Olivia's position.

"My goodness, it's cold," Olivia said, stomping her feet on the floor as she came in, the wind blowing in behind her.

He reached over and helped her shut the door, then took the box of candles from her arms.

"I'll show you how those work in a minute, but I don't want to hold you up."

"I would like to get around and see if there's anyone else who needs a ride to the church. I know that Noah and Ben are helping to gather people up, but I want to do my part as well."

"That's fine. I won't light the candles until you're able to look at them."

"No. If you think that they'll work, you go right ahead."

"I just thought that if the lights were dim, and people needed a little bit of a welcoming glow, the candles would give it."

"I trust you. You be in charge of that."

She smiled when he said he trusted her, and their eyes met again. He wanted to reach out, to touch her shoulder, or run his finger down her cheek. But he didn't. Instead, he let his look speak all the words he couldn't, before he turned around and walked back out into the storm.

Chapter Twelve

"You can put that over here on the table," Marjorie McBride said, as she directed her son, Roland, as he carried a great big pot of what Olivia was guessing to be soup in his hands.

"Olivia, grab some bowls from the kitchen and some spoons while you're at it."

Olivia nodded, noticing that Marjorie kept her voice pitched low, because some of the people who had come in were lying on the floor sleeping. Aiden and Ethan thankfully had gone back to sleep, cuddled in a corner that Olivia had set up for the three of them, although she hadn't laid down herself.

She had been busy with the candles until Marjorie came in, and now it looked like she was going to help hand out soup.

"That smells delicious," she said as Roland set the big pot down and Marjorie lifted the lid.

"I hope it's good. When I realized how bad the storm was going to be, I went to work. If only we had homemade bread."

"If I get some time, I can put some together." Making homemade bread had been one of her favorite things to do before Cam died and she had to put all of her time and effort into the candle shop and making a living.

"I'll try to make sure you get time, because I think that would go just as far toward making people feel calm and comfortable."

Olivia nodded, and then walked on into the kitchen, not sure where the disposable bowls that Marjorie was talking about were kept. But she wasn't afraid to look and started opening up cupboard doors. The fourth one she opened was the jackpot, and she grabbed a big stack of disposable bowls. It wasn't hard to find the spoons, and she was back out while Marjorie was still bustling around, directing her boys to set another big pot of stew down and what looked like a vegetable tray.

"You and Pastor Mark should've coordinated. He's got vegetables as well. As well as fruit."

"Well, good. I figure as long as we keep people's bellies full, they'll be less likely to be irritated with each other."

Olivia nodded, never having considered that people might get irritated with each other. But Marjorie was probably right, and her foresight born of experience. After all, people almost always found things to squabble over, and in a place like this where they couldn't get away from each other for possibly days on end, there were bound to be short tempers.

"We want to make sure we keep the bathrooms tidy and clean as well. I think food and bathrooms are probably going to be our biggest concerns. Although, keeping people from getting bored might be a problem." She seemed like she was thinking to herself. Then she seemed to shake herself out of it, and she said, "How about you come around here and use this ladle to dip vegetable soup out. I'll use this ladle for the chicken noodle soup."

"All right," Olivia said.

"I see your boys sleeping over there in the corner. If they wake up, we'll find someone to replace you."

"I think they'll probably sleep until morning. Although, they're not used to getting woken up in the middle of the night the way they were today, so who knows what they'll do."

"Just when we think we have our kids figured out, they throw us a curveball. I know how that goes," Marjorie said.

"I'm sure you do. Raising all the kids that you did. You did such a great job. All of your children are in church and serving the Lord. I feel like you need to write a book."

Marjorie laughed. "I don't feel like I have anything to say. It was only through the grace of God. Of course, I can relate to you, since I lost my husband as well." She paused, and then she said, "My kids weren't quite that little."

"Yeah. I don't know whether it's easier or harder that the kids have no memories of him at all. They weren't even born when he died."

"It's probably easier. They don't know what they're missing. But it's harder for you, because you don't have anyone to share your memories with." Marjorie sighed. "The kids and I talk about their dad all the time. Not that he was perfect, but when someone passes away, you have a tendency to look back with rose-colored glasses. At least I do."

Olivia nodded, looking over at the other people milling about. There were probably twenty adults and maybe not quite that many children. Several of the adults were elderly and sat in the camp chairs, rather than trying to get down on the floor.

"I sent Roland to go get the cots that we have in the barn. I covered them with a blanket years ago. We haven't used them since the kids have gotten older, but that might work better than having some of these older folks trying to get down on the floor. I know I could get down, but I'm not sure I can get myself back up at this point in my life." Marjorie laughed.

"You're looking a lot better than you have for a while," Olivia said, not sure whether Marjorie was talking about the cancer that she'd gone through. For a long time, there were rumors that swirled around her that she might have diabetes or something else. But she hadn't announced it, and it seemed to be something she wanted to keep secret.

"Thank you. There for a while I wasn't sure whether I really wanted to live. I had time to contemplate the idea that I probably wasn't going to."

"Weren't you scared?" Olivia couldn't help but ask.

Marjorie waited until Mrs. Biddle, who had come up for soup, left with a bowl of vegetable soup cradled in her hands, before she said, "I suppose at times I was. The middle of the night when you wake up and you can't breathe, or you're in a lot of pain and you wonder if this is it, you know?"

"What did you do?"

"I just reminded myself that heaven was going to be better than now. It's hard to let go of the idea that we want to live, because God created us with that drive. But He also promises to be with us, to walk with us all the time, and I assume that means even in death. So therefore, I would just say, 'Jesus, I'm scared. Remember your promise to stay with me? I'm gonna cling to you. Because I don't know how to die.'" Marjorie laughed. There wasn't a whole lot of humor in it, but her face looked relaxed and at peace. "Isn't that the fear? It's the unknown? I don't know what dying is going to entail. Is it going to hurt? And of course I'm going to be scared. Anytime you can't breathe, or you feel a lot of pain, it's scary. So I think that's normal. And I would remind myself of that too. But," here she gave a little laugh, "just look at graveyards. How many millions, or billions of people have died before me? They've all somehow gotten through it. I can do it too, I guess."

"I've never thought about it that way. I suppose my husband has died, and he managed it. I guess I can do it if he can." Olivia couldn't help but laugh, because it seemed like convoluted logic in some way, but it was true. If her husband could do it, if her grandparents could die, so could she. Not that she would have a choice.

"I don't know why we're so scared of dying. There are a lot of things that are worse than dying. A lot of sins that we just wink at, that if we really could see the world through God's eyes, we would see that sin as far, far worse than death. We get hung up on things that don't matter."

"I'm guilty of that. I don't need to think about death in order to know it isn't the worst thing that could happen to me."

"But I will tell you that coming face-to-face with death, and having to come to grips with it... it changed me. Maybe made me more determined to use the time that I have left to serve people to the best of my ability. To try to show them Jesus, however I can. To actually live what I say I believe, because so often I don't."

"Well, that's a surprise to me. It's not hard for me to see Jesus when I look at you."

"You can't see my thoughts. If you could, if they could be displayed right there on the wall for everyone to read, I would be so embarrassed. I would rather be out in that blowing wind and blistering cold than sitting in here knowing everybody knew what I thought today. And that's just today."

Olivia nodded. "I would be out there with you, if my thoughts were on the wall."

Thoughts about Pastor Mark. She hadn't been able to get him out of her head since she had left after checking out the rec room and seeing how well prepared he was. And yet, he had admitted to her that he was afraid that he wouldn't be able to hold up to Pastor Johnson's standards, and people would be disappointed in him. Such a talented man, so thoughtful, and so concerned about people, and yet... he didn't think he was good enough. He was humble and capable and caring and protective. How he carried her boys in. She loved how gentle he was with them, how easily he spoke with them, despite not having children of his own.

Marjorie had served two more people, and she didn't seem to notice that Olivia's thoughts had gone off the rails.

And then, the object of her thoughts opened the door and came in with a gust of wind, his arm around an elderly woman who had taken the time to get completely dressed, put a scarf over her head, and a coat bundled up around her.

"Oh good. He thought to check on Mrs. Richardson. She's by herself and just about a mile outside of town."

"Yeah, in that trailer by herself. I bet she lost electricity before the rest of us did."

"I bet she did too, and I bet Pastor will be over here to get her some soup. She looks cold."

Olivia nodded, as she spooned out more soup for two of Marjorie's grandchildren. Marjorie chatted with them a bit, and then they went back over to where their mother had sleeping bags and a couple of chairs set up for them.

Each family seemed to take a little spot for themselves, spacing their areas out so that no one was sitting on top of anyone else.

"I was afraid we might have some squabbles, because when you get too many people together for too long, especially if they don't have anything productive to do, they have a tendency to find anything and everything to disagree about."

Marjorie laughed. "Boy, you are correct about that. But maybe the fact that we're in the church, that Pastor is here walking around looking at everyone, that we just feel a little bit closer to God here. Maybe that'll help keep us in line." And then she shook her head with a grunt. "Or not." Her eyes twinkled as they met Olivia's. Both of them knew that Marjorie was probably engaging in wishful thinking.

"Reminds me of what Paul says in Corinthians where he says the things that he doesn't want to do, he ends up doing, and the things that he does want to do, he doesn't. I can stand here and say I'm not going to argue with anyone, but... just let someone mistreat my children, and I'll be at their throat in no time. It will take me a little while to remind myself that I wasn't going to act like that. And then I'll be embarrassed."

"Our children really bring out the mother bears in us. I admit to flying off the handle a few times when I shouldn't have, that's for sure."

"Will it ever get better? Because I'm trying. But it seems like I fail constantly."

"I know this is where I'm supposed to say that it's not supposed to be you, it's supposed to be Jesus, but I've always been of the mind that it takes both of you. After all, God commands us to be holy. If He gives us that command, surely there's something that we need to do, actively. But we also know that we can't do anything without the Lord's help. So, I've always figured that it's one hundred percent me and one hundred percent God. And sometimes we grow in some areas more slowly than others." She lifted a shoulder. "I know I've been working on some things for decades, and I'm still working on them. God has helped, but... I'm not where I'd like to be. In fact, it seems like the older I get, the more I see that I'm so far away from what I'd like to be, that it feels like I'll never get there."

"In heaven," Olivia said. "We'll be there in heaven."

"That was another reason why I was kind of looking forward to it. After all, I've been striving for years to try to be holy, and in heaven, all of my efforts will be realized."

"$\mathcal{D}$r. Terry and I are making sure that at least one of us is on call the entire time we're here. We do have a generator at the clinic, but it doesn't run the entire thing, just the refrigerators and some backup lights."

"It makes sense for you guys to move your operations here, although obviously it would not be normal operations," Pastor Mark said, appreciating the fact that people had been taking it upon themselves to contribute where they felt they could.

"And I have coordinated with the department to make sure that I'm able to be here to respond to any issues," Ben said, his arm around Hannah, the closeness of their bodies saying without words their comfortableness toward each other.

"I appreciate that."

"As long as the roads remain passable, I'll be checking on people. But if we get as much snow as what they're calling for, that's not going to last the entire time."

"No. And so far everything has been worse than what they've said, so I don't know why that wouldn't be too." Mark didn't believe in being all gloom and doom all the time, but it was true that when things started going south, they usually went south in a hurry and further south than anyone anticipated. That was just being real, not negative. At least he told himself that.

His eyes drifted across the room where Olivia stood dishing soup out and chatting with Marjorie McBride. He couldn't think of a better person to be talking to her. Marjorie was full of wisdom and kindness, and she was just one of those people that anyone could learn something from. A person didn't have to be in her presence very long before her wisdom started rubbing off.

The church could use a hundred more people like Marjorie.

Of course, everyone had their place, and God had a place for everyone.

"If you have a moment, Pastor, I had an idea," Noah said, interrupting Mark's thoughts.

He nodded at Ben and Hannah as they moved away, confident that any medical emergencies would be taken care of, and that Ben would keep things in order, and also make sure that anyone intent on no good would not get in to harm his congregation.

After all, it would be defeating the purpose to lock the doors.

"I'm all yours." He turned and faced Noah fully. Noah stood with his wife, Grace. His arm was around her, but both of her eyes were on him.

"I was already working on music for Christmas, but since we have everyone here, and I assume that people are going to be a little bit bored and maybe restless, I was wondering if it might be okay to see if we can put together a musical performance. Something we can do maybe between Christmas and New Year's, a town thing, but considering that this is church property, I thought I'd get your permission."

"You certainly have my permission." He paused for a moment, thinking about how he had just been thinking about how everyone had their place. There was Noah, donating what he had.

"But?" Noah prompted, as though knowing that Mark had more to say.

"I've had this thought in my head for a while, but I don't know if it's doable on such short notice."

"We're gonna have a lot of time. What's your idea?" Noah asked, looking excited about the challenge.

"I've seen multiple candlelight musical performances. Some with dancing, some with just music, and they always look so magical. I don't know if it's too late for us to do something like that or not?"

He also thought that would give Olivia more business, if they were able to buy the candles from her. He would suggest it if Noah didn't.

Noah glanced over his shoulder. His wife said, "Olivia is here. We can ask her if it would be possible to have... How many candles would that take?" She paused. "I know we could get the musical part down."

Noah nodded. "I agree. Even if we use some of the music that we've already done this season, the candlelight would make it special in a way that it wasn't before."

"The snow would add that magical touch as well."

"And we could clear off an area around the church to do it outside. Although we could practice inside. We wouldn't need to practice the candlelight, of course."

"No, but we might need to figure out how we're going to set them up and light those candles. That might be the thing."

They stood there thinking for a moment, and then Pastor Mark said, "Maybe we should just ask Olivia. She might not be able to get that many candles, although she might be able to estimate how many candles we would need. If she can provide them, she might have an idea about how to light them."

"She is the expert in this area. But with your blessing, maybe I can coordinate with her." Noah seemed thoughtful. Then he said to Pastor, "I'd like to have a short message. Nothing terribly long, but just enough so that people who maybe normally don't go to church might hear the gospel."

"I could do that. Make it non-threatening. Thank you for thinking of that."

"The older I get, the more I realize that the point of my life here is not to make myself happy, but to live for Jesus. It's funny how that becomes more urgent with every passing year."

"Some Christians never get that urgency. And I don't understand why. If you truly believe that Jesus saves, and He saved you from eternity in hell, wouldn't you be desperate to tell as many people as you could?"

He never understood that. But he supposed that was why he ended up being a pastor, because he couldn't shake that urgency, even from his youngest years. Other people didn't seem to be bothered by it at all, which was hard for Mark to comprehend.

"I don't want to take you from other duties if you're busy, Pastor, but if you're not, we could go over and talk to Olivia now." Noah looked at him with a studied gaze that didn't seem to have any ulterior motives.

Mark wasn't sure why that thought struck him, but it did.

Maybe it was because he was eager to go over and talk to Olivia.

"Absolutely. I'm excited about this idea. I've always wanted to put on one of these with the candlelight, and you're right, this is the perfect time to practice."

"But if Olivia doesn't have candles already made, she might have trouble coming up with as many as we need in as short of time as what we need them."

"Yeah. That would be disappointing, but not surprising," Mark said. But he knew that she could use the money. And he was excited that they could give her the work. He just didn't know how she could get it all done.

Unless someone helped her.

Christmas was his busiest time of year, other than possibly Easter. And especially since he was just starting out, he really shouldn't take the time. But the idea of giving Olivia a hand stuck in his brain.

The three of them walked across the floor, greeting people as they went, smelling the delicious smells of the soup rising around them.

For now, people were content and happy, although he could tell that there were some anxious ones among them.

He didn't see any point in getting upset about things. There wasn't anything they could do now while the storm raged around them. The time for looking to see what they could do to fix it would come later. It could be a lot of work. So they might as well enjoy their time off now.

"Hey, Mrs. McBride, do you mind if we steal your helper for a minute?" Noah said, charming Mrs. McBride with a boyish grin.

"I suppose. Then bring her back. We were having a great conversation."

"I enjoy talking to you. I'll definitely be back," Olivia said, patting Mrs. McBride on the arm before she smoothed down her apron and came around the table.

"What can I do to help you guys?" she asked, and Mark figured that she probably had no idea what she was about to get into.

"I'll let Pastor explain," Noah said, exchanging a look with his wife that Mark couldn't read.

"All right." He turned and faced Olivia fully, glancing around to make sure they weren't being overheard. There was no point in announcing it before they were sure they were going to be able to pull it off.

And packed together the way everyone was, rumors were bound to swirl.

"We have an idea, but we're going to need your help to pull it off."

Olivia's brows went up, but she waited, giving him time to speak.

He went over what he and Noah had talked about, and then said, "How many candles do you think that will take?"

"I was just trying to figure that out. It would really depend on what we do. If we're going to try to fill up the entire parking lot with candles, I'm not sure that will work. But if we had the musicians on a platform and had candles to finish filling the platform up, that might be a little bit more doable." She glanced at Noah. "How soon were you planning on putting this on?"

Mark realized he hadn't mentioned that when he was explaining exactly what they were doing.

"I was hoping between Christmas and New Year's."

Olivia's eyes got huge. Mark could almost see her thinking to herself that she needed the work, but that she didn't know whether she could pull that off or not.

"If you guys don't mind, I just realized that people might not have brought their instruments to the church. Let me go see if we have enough people to even practice something like this," Noah said, and his wife nodded.

"I hadn't even thought about that. Although we do have some extra instruments..." And they walked off, discussing the logistics of the music.

"I'm sorry, I didn't mean to put you on the spot like that. I can tell from the expression on your face that you probably are thinking that you're not going to be able to pull it off."

"I wish I could. This would be huge. And beautiful. I've always wanted to do something like this. And I have just the design that I've been working on."

"Do you have any extra candles sitting around?"

"I guess we did talk about that. They would not match, though. They'd be an eclectic mix, and I'm not sure how that would look." Her voice seemed to trail off as she thought about it.

"Well, I'm no expert on candles, but we could use a specific design around the instrumentalists to try to keep the fire hazard down, but in the open areas, we could have a different kind of candle. Or something like that?" Mark was thinking as he spoke, and he probably shouldn't have even made suggestions. What did he know about candles and the artistic arrangement of them?

"That's a great idea! And if we did it like that, I might actually not have to make nearly as many candles as what I was just thinking."

"I think anything would be beautiful. And... I can help."

She blinked, and her eyes widened as she looked at him.

"You would?"

"Yeah. Noah left before we said anything, but he had asked if I would give a presentation of the gospel for the people who are there, and I'm invested in it now. So helping you would be part of my job, actually."

She laughed a little, as he had intended. There was something about her laugh that just made him feel good the whole way down to his toes and back.

"Well, that sounds logical to me. Are you sure you don't mind?" she asked, and he appreciated the fact that she wanted to be sure that she wasn't taking advantage of him. A lot of people assumed that since he was a pastor, they could get away with a lot more than they could with a regular person, because after all, he was commanded to be kind and not mean. And they expected him to live by that. Interestingly, the commands for him were no greater than the commands for regular Christians, but it was Christians who expected him to be held to a higher standard.

"Are you sure we'll be able to get it done? I'm not sure how long we'll be sidelined by the storm."

"That is a concern. But yeah, as long as I have a week, I think I'll be fine. It'll be a hectic week, and I probably won't sleep much, but as long as I have some time off to spend Christmas with my boys, it'll be good."

He nodded. "They come first. And they're good kids too."

"They seem to be able to finagle their way into a lot of situations that I could not. I should blame Aiden, because Ethan usually just goes along."

"I think most relationships have people like that. They're hardly ever equal. One is a go-getter, and one is more content to stay behind and be the support." Their eyes met, and he wished he knew what she was thinking.

Was it about the kind of couple that she and her husband had been?

"We've got enough musicians to practice," Noah said, before Mark could change the subject in any way. Not that he wanted to. This was not the place to talk about stuff like that. Even if he did want his relationship with Olivia to be a little bit more than what it was.

Was that what he wanted?

He needed to find out what she wanted before he got so emotionally attached that he wasn't able to make logical decisions. He'd seen that happen over and over again—people who were not compatible at all forming relationships and getting married just because they were doing what their emotions dictated. When anyone who looked at them knew that it probably wasn't going to last.

Not that he ever wanted to have such negative views of anything. After all, he was a firm believer that God could take anything and make something out of it.

"That's great. I was just trying to figure out how many candles you would need and whether or not I would be able to get it done, but Pastor said he would help me, and I actually think that it's doable."

"That's great!" Noah said, looking excited. Grace stood beside him.

"Are you sure? I don't want you to not sleep for the entire week of Christmas because you're working your fingers to the bone."

Olivia shook her head at Grace. "No. I think it's totally doable, and I'm excited about it. It sounds like it will be beautiful, and I'm thrilled and honored that I will get to play a small part in it."

"We haven't actually talked about the cost. I assumed that we would charge money for tickets and be able to pay for the candles that way. I guess I hadn't gotten any further than that." Noah looked a little sheepish, like he should've thought of such things.

"I'm not too concerned about it. I will use some candles I already have, and while I can definitely use the work and the money, I understand this is a spur-of-the-moment thing."

"But we've got a captive audience right here, and we can sell tickets to all of them, and also make some announcements on social media and online. We can even use the church's website to announce it as well."

"All right then. I'll figure some things out and we'll get together to make those announcements." Grace smiled. And then, talking to each other, they walked off.

"They work so well together," Olivia said. And then she shook her head, and glanced at him and gave a nervous laugh. He got the feeling that she hadn't meant for him to hear that.

"I think some people just do. They click or something, you know? Not that a marriage can't happen between two people who don't get along, don't work well together to begin with. I think that's something you grow into eventually if you don't have it to begin with."

"I agree. It's always nice when that happens."

Again, he wanted to ask about her previous relationship, but he knew this was not the time.

"I probably ought to make some rounds, but I'll check in with you in a little bit. And if I don't see you again tonight, I'll see you in the morning."

"All right. Sounds good," she said. She took a step toward the tables where the soup was, and then she turned back and said, "Thanks a lot for this, for the candlelight service. I appreciate that."

He wasn't sure exactly what she was saying. Whether or not she knew that he had pretty much finagled both of those things for her, thinking of her and hoping to help her. Or whether she was just excited to be a part of it. He wasn't sure, but he simply nodded and said, "It's just a small-town thing."

"It's a God thing," she corrected him before she turned and left.

Yeah. It was a God thing. And he loved that she saw it. The more time he spent with her, the more he felt like she would be a perfect pastor's wife, but it had to be something she wanted. Not something that he forced her into. Like the couples who worked well together. It might not be smooth sailing at first, all the time, but there had to be a want-to from both of them.

Lord, I don't want to jump the gun if this isn't what you want. Please show me.

Chapter Fourteen

"There, all washed and ready to be filled up tomorrow," Marjorie said, wiping her hands on her apron as Olivia put the large kettle upside down on the counter.

"I can't believe we used all of that soup. I never dreamed we would eat it all."

"I think sometimes when things like this happen, all people have to do is sit around and eat. And a full belly definitely keeps people happier anyway."

Olivia laughed. She had to agree with that.

She noticed that Pastor Mark had gone around to each family, talking to them, praying with some of them, and seeming to ease everyone's fears.

Still, as late as it was—almost midnight from what she could figure—there was still a lot of activity going on. It was like people couldn't settle down.

"Olivia, can I have a word with you, please?"

She turned to see Mark standing in the doorway, his brows raised in question.

"Of course. Excuse me, Mrs. McBride."

"After today, please call me Marjorie. There's no need to stand on ceremony."

"Of course, Marjorie. You're just so wise, I feel like a child compared to you."

"Oh, fiddlesticks. When you get to be my age, you'll be just as wise. The fear of the Lord is the beginning of wisdom."

"I'll remember that," she said as she walked away. The storm was not a good thing in most ways that people counted good things—but for the most part, she was grateful that she got to spend so much time with Marjorie.

"A very wise woman," Pastor Mark said as they walked out of the kitchen area and over to an area where there weren't many people around.

"I thought people would be settling down by now," Pastor Mark said.

"I was surprised at how many people are still up too." She lifted a shoulder, unsure what more they could do to settle things down.

"I wanted to ask if it would be okay if we used all of the candles to kind of make a circle. I want to be careful, because obviously we do not want to risk a fire. But I was going to dim the lights, use the candles, and have a prayer service. I think people could really use that right now. They seem to be anxious and on edge, and unable to just let it go and let God do what He's going to do, and to trust Him."

"Of course. I can help."

"You've been dishing out soup for the last several hours. I would like to see you get off of your feet for a bit."

"I will, as soon as I get the candles lit, okay? You set them around wherever you want to, and I'll light them."

"All right. Sounds like a plan."

She realized that she had basically hijacked him and told him what to do. But he rolled with it. If that was what he was planning all along, he didn't say.

Maybe she did have a tendency to grab the bull by the horns. After all, the last few years that she'd spent on her own, having to figure things out, having to take care of herself and her boys, had taught her that she couldn't be a shrinking violet.

But maybe she could learn to do that again. To support rather than command. She would like that.

Mark arranged the candles cleverly, so that there was no chance of having them knocked over, but that they would provide the maximum amount of warmth and glowing light for the group of people who gathered. He made a small announcement, quiet, so that he didn't wake any of the sleeping congregants, but loud enough that everyone could hear. Soon there were fifteen or so people gathered around, sitting in the chairs that he had arranged.

"I feel a little restless tonight," he began, as Olivia sat down in a chair in the back. She had to admit it felt good to be off her feet. But she also loved listening to Mark. His voice was calm and soothing, yet he had a commanding air about him that wasn't arrogant or intimidating. Just... comforting. The kind of man a person felt like they could trust. "And I thought it might be a nice idea for us all to get together and just reaffirm the fact that God is in control, and that we trust Him to have our very best at heart. Even if that sometimes hurts in the present moment."

There were nods around, and Olivia found herself agreeing as well. It was hard to trust. Especially when bad things were happening that a person had no control over, but they knew God could stop if He wanted to, and yet God chose not to.

"I don't understand why God lets bad things happen to good people."

Olivia wasn't sure, but that sounded like Millie Sanderson.

"That's just it. God's ways are higher than our ways. That's what it says in Isaiah. And his thoughts are higher than our thoughts. And that's why it's important for us to trust him. Because while we can't understand, and we don't see why, God does." Pastor Mark looked around the group. "He sees the whole picture. Not just the little pieces that we see. After all, when you have a puzzle to put together and you have one blue piece, you don't judge the whole thing, thinking you know what the whole puzzle should be just based on that piece. Do you?"

"No, of course we don't."

"And that's the way life is. We just see the little part that we're living. And not even all of that, a lot of times. After all, how many times have you lost something that you just had in your hand a few moments ago, and can't find it anywhere?"

There was a murmur of laughter. "So if we can't even keep track of our little day-to-day things, how can we even pretend to know or think we know what God should be doing? When we can't see it all."

"But I know when it hurts. And losing work right now, having the roof of my house cave in, that's gonna hurt."

Olivia couldn't see who spoke, but it was true. Losing the business this close to Christmas was going to pinch her financially. Although, God had already made a way for her to make more than she would've made had she been open on a regular year.

"Sometimes I think that's the whole 'God closes a door but he opens a window.' We think it should happen so that we're not inconvenienced or hurt at all, but it's usually in those times of inconvenience where we grow the most. And isn't that what God wants? For us to grow?" Pastor looked around, and there were a few nods, although Olivia noticed that there were a few people who didn't want to admit that. She could be in that camp. After all, for years, she'd questioned why God had her husband die. And she still didn't understand.

"That's what the Bible means when it says that we're supposed to trust God like a little child. You don't see Olivia's twin boys over there asking their mommy why they have to sleep at the church. They just get excited about the new thing."

"That's because they can't see how damaging it could be to our business," one guy spoke up.

"It's true. And maybe sometimes we see things, and we should just let them go. Because that's not our concern. If we can't do anything about it, if there's nothing we can do, let it go. Let God worry about it. The Bible says His yoke is easy and His burden light. We're supposed to cast our cares on Him. He doesn't want us carrying around those things that are too heavy for us. We get bowed under the weight of those things, and then we're miserable, first of all, and secondly, He can't use us the way He wants to. Because when we're carrying around all of those encumbrances, we can't use our hands and our backs for God's work, because we're stuck carrying things around that we shouldn't be."

"That's good. Preach it," one lady murmured.

Mark smiled just a little, but he looked over his small group, and Olivia could almost feel the love burning in his heart for the people that God had called him to shepherd.

His eyes met hers for a brief moment, and maybe it was just her imagination, but she felt like there was something special between them.

But his eyes moved on, and the feeling was gone.

"That's what faith is. Simple trust. And we're trusting God for our eternity, right? At least we say we do. We say we're trusting Him to keep us out of hell, to take us to heaven. How can we not trust Him with a little storm? It's our whole world, but most of this country is not getting snowed on right now. It seems like a huge thing to us. But it's not nearly as big as eternity, or even as a soul getting saved."

There was silence there, as though people were trying to make the connections.

She had to admit that Mark was good at speaking off the cuff. He didn't have any notes with him, and he wasn't even holding a Bible.

"Trust in the Lord with all thine heart and lean not unto thine own understanding. In all thy ways acknowledge him, and he shall direct thy paths. In everything we do, we're supposed to acknowledge God. And everything that happens to us, we're to trust. It sounds simple, but... I don't know about you, but I've spent more than a few minutes a little worried tonight."

"Why would you worry? This is your house. If anything's gonna survive the storm, it's gonna be you. Plus, you're working overtime. But most of us aren't working at all."

There was a murmur of laughter around, and Mark nodded.

"I was a little worried there might be a fight breaking out. Or something like that."

"Yeah, I don't know if Eleanor and Casey can be in the same room for more than an hour together before they start to fight. They should've gotten married back when they could've. And now the rest of us have had to deal with their antagonistic attitudes for the last thirty years."

Olivia didn't know where Casey was, but she could see Eleanor with her arms crossed over her chest, although she smiled a little, as though acknowledging the truth of those words.

"He's not here, so you don't have to worry about me getting into a fistfight," she said when the laughter died down. But her words inspired more laughter.

"Well, there's a relief. And see? I could've just trusted God to take care of that, but instead I had to worry about it."

"Well, I'm not saying anything about anybody else. I'm just talking about me," Eleanor clarified. Everyone shook their heads, hoping the town could get along for the duration of the storm.

Chapter Fifteen

Mark woke in the predawn darkness, immediately wide awake. He'd fallen asleep praying for everyone in the shelter and those he knew were weathering the storm without coming in.

He started his day the same way he'd ended it, praying for the people under his care, and that God would help him to shepherd them well and to help him become more like Jesus, so he could point them to the Savior.

He slipped out of his bed, still praying, but restless. Normally, when he prayed in the morning, he paced around the church, although he did spend time on his knees before the Lord.

He carefully mapped out where everyone was the night before and managed to avoid stepping on anyone as he headed to the kitchen to grab a glass of water.

He hadn't wanted to sleep in his own bed. The parsonage was separate from the church, and the generator only provided electricity for the church, so even though his house was right next door and connected via his office, it was cold and dark.

"I'm sorry. I didn't realize you were up," Olivia said, as he almost ran into her coming out of the kitchen as he was going in.

"No. I'm sorry. I..." He looked around, and then jerked his head back toward the kitchen. He didn't want their speaking to wake anyone up. It probably wasn't even quite five o'clock yet.

She jerked her head in return and went back into the kitchen.

He carefully closed the door behind him, and with the light on over the stove, he could see that she still wore pajamas, and her hair didn't look like it had been brushed.

"Just getting up for a drink?" he asked, although she didn't owe him any explanations. It wasn't like he was the movement police or anything.

She didn't seem offended as she shook her head.

"No. I always wake up early. I didn't used to. I would've considered myself more of a night owl, but after the twins came, the only time all day that I was guaranteed to have any kind of personal, private time was first thing in the morning. It got to where I felt like I needed that, to just spend time with the Lord and center myself for the day I was going to have."

"It couldn't have been easy raising two boys by yourself."

"No."

She didn't say anything else, and he didn't pressure her.

"I guess we have that in common then," he said. "Although I never did consider myself a night owl. I'm definitely not one now. I actually slept in a little this morning."

"It was a big day yesterday."

He nodded. "But I thought it went well. Hopefully today goes just as well. I haven't checked. Is it still snowing?" He glanced out the window but couldn't really tell. The streetlights were off.

"Yes. I opened the door just to see how deep it was, and I'd say we've got a foot, maybe closer to eighteen inches."

"Wow. It's not messing around."

"No. I glanced at the weather on my phone, and it said it should be ending this evening."

"How much are we supposed to get in the meantime?"

"We could get up to another two feet," she said, shuddering.

He sighed.

"Are you okay?" she asked, stepping closer and putting a hand on his forearm.

He felt her nearness like a comforting blanket. And her hand on his arm felt steady and warm.

"Yeah. I guess I just... I worry that I'm not going to live up to what Pastor Johnson was, you know?"

He didn't even realize he was going to say something like that. But it was true. So much of him wondered if the church people were looking at him and finding him lacking.

"I don't think you need to worry about that."

"He was so much wiser than I am. Sometimes wisdom is just something that you gain with age, the more time you spend with God. And I don't have as much as he did. I don't have the time with the Lord that he did, and maybe I don't have the heart for people. Maybe I don't have what it takes to lead a bigger congregation. My last church was really small."

"If this is where God called you, this is the job that he wants for you—it doesn't matter whether you think you're qualified or not. God will give you what you need. And whatever you are is exactly what you need to be right here in this moment."

He stared at her. He knew all of that. She wasn't telling him anything that he didn't know. He just forgot sometimes. Needed someone to point him back to God and the Bible. Not to give in to his fears and give voice to his insecurities and tell him that they were normal. They were, of course. Every great man of God had times where he despaired or was depressed or felt fear. Wondered where God was, even.

"Thank you. I needed that reminder," he finally said, still wondering where she got the wisdom to set him straight. "I think most people wouldn't have said that to me."

"I guess I'm not most people," she said, lifting a shoulder. "Honestly, I'm a little scared myself. After all, I got the last-minute Christmas candlelight service order to do. And then, yesterday I just agreed to do another huge order. I don't even know if I'm going to get paid for that one. We talked about sales and tickets and that type of thing, but I know that they're starting this with no money. So if they don't make anything, am I gonna demand that I still get paid? After all, the idea was partly mine. I should take a little risk too. But at the same time, I can't really afford to lose a whole lot." She paused, and then she said, "But through it all, I know that God's going to take care of me. I know that."

"That's great. So many people just don't have that kind of trust. I hear people say, 'Where is God? Why is he allowing me to go through this?'"

"I don't really question that about my actual life. Not too much anyway. Because I know that God didn't put me here on earth to have a life of ease and luxury. He wants me to work for him. But he also wants to grow my faith, and test it some."

"That's true. I think, especially in our American way, we've lost sight of the idea that life isn't about us and our comfort and our security and our ease and our prosperity. The prosperity gospel probably has something to do with that."

"Yeah. There are grains of truth in it, and it can be very helpful for some people, but it also makes it when bad things happen, people doubt God."

He couldn't believe that they were so aligned on that issue. It was rare for him to find men of God who were so grounded in the truth, and yet here was this woman in front of him who seemed perfectly at ease discussing it with him. And he couldn't deny the bit of attraction that had been flowing between them. Whether she felt it too, he didn't know.

At some point, her hand had dropped off his arm, but he was so focused on what she was saying that he hadn't noticed.

"You probably shouldn't get me started. I could go on all day about the things that modern Christians believe that aren't biblical at all."

"We could go on all day together then, because I have a few pet peeves myself. Not the least of which is that we have to put up with sin, when God clearly said that we're to hate sin. And that we are to strive to be holy."

"Oh yeah, people think that they shouldn't be doing anything to be holy, that God will do it all. And I guess I would have to challenge those people, because I don't see that anywhere in the Bible. Man always has to follow God by faith before God works. That's the formula. It requires a deliberate choice and action on our part."

"Agreed. I have to say I'm impressed."

"With what?" she asked, sounding truly surprised.

How did he say it? At her wisdom? At her knowledge of the Bible? And how what she believed aligned with what he did?

Maybe he waited too long to say anything, because beside him, Olivia shifted.

"I better get back to the boys. They're not usually up this early, but if they do get up, I don't want them to wake anyone else."

"No. Of course not."

She didn't make any move to leave, though, and he felt like there was more that they needed to say to each other.

"It was good to talk to you. I appreciate that," he finally said.

"Yeah, it was nice to voice my concerns, I guess. Sometimes just talking about things makes them smaller in my eyes."

"It's funny. Some people need to talk about things, some people need to internalize them and roll them over that way."

"Yeah. My husband was one of those internals. He didn't say much."

"My parents were both like that. Neither one of them talked a whole lot, and I think they assumed that I knew things I didn't."

She didn't say anything, and he remembered that there seemed to be some kind of issue between her and her parents.

"Are your parents coming in for Christmas?" he asked.

"No."

She didn't elaborate. He wanted to push, to ask for more, but they'd already talked about their vulnerabilities, and he didn't want to pry.

"If you want to talk about it, I'm available."

She nodded, and then she turned and walked to the door.

He waited until after she left, thinking about their conversation, about the things that she said, and how she encouraged him, making him feel like he was just enough for the job at hand. Reminding him that God called him here, so therefore whatever he had was exactly right.

He had needed to hear that.

Lord, thank you for that reminder today, even though it came from a person, not from your word.

He walked over to the door, opening it and looking out.

Olivia had been right. There was at least a foot or a foot and a half of snow out, and it was still coming down hard. The wind had died down, though, so maybe the crews would be able to get out and work on getting the electricity back. It had to be wind damage, since they didn't have that much snow when it went out.

Somehow, the idea of not being around Olivia anymore made him wish that the storm would drag on and the crews would be slow today.

Chapter Sixteen

"I was thinking the musicians could sit here at these X's, and where I have the circles would be candles," Olivia said as she talked to Grace about the seating arrangement for the candlelight concert. Musicians had been practicing all day, while she had been mostly busy in the kitchen, helping Marjorie make more pots of soup.

She'd also baked two dozen loaves of bread. Her arms felt like spaghetti, but she wanted to keep her mind active.

Ethan and Aiden loved having other children to play with, and Isadora McBride had had activities for the children all day long. Her three children had helped her, and Olivia felt like she had a lot in common with Isadora. Although Isadora's husband had cheated on her and left her, they still were single moms, raising active children. She thought Isadora was doing an excellent job, since her children seemed well-adjusted and happy. But maybe that had something to do with the fact that the McBride family stuck together, and while there was no father in their immediate family, Isadora had multiple brothers and brothers-in-law who would fill that role for her kids.

Olivia pressed her lips together and tried to pay attention to what Grace was saying. She didn't have siblings, and she wasn't talking to her parents.

Maybe that was a mistake. That wasn't the first time she'd thought it, but she didn't usually allow those thoughts in. Because that would mean that she needed to reach out, apologize, ask for forgiveness, and overlook the things that they had done to her.

She wasn't sure she was ready for that yet. After all, she didn't feel like it was her fault.

Those were all uncomfortable things that she didn't want to face. It was easier to put all of her attention into baking bread, making candles, and designing seating arrangements.

"I think we probably ought to move one of these chairs over here. It would look more symmetrical that way, and folks on the side would be able to see the candles better."

"Oh. Yes. That's a great shift. I was also hoping we could have the platform raised a little, but I know that we're getting close to the deadline, and I don't know if that type of construction is possible."

"I might be able to talk to Jude and a couple of the McBride boys. They're pretty handy, and they might be able to knock this together in an afternoon. Although, we might have to buy the lumber for it. And that's another expense."

"How are the ticket sales going?" Olivia had been afraid to ask, but she figured she'd better just bite the bullet and find out.

"If the quote that you gave us for the candles is accurate, we only need to sell a few more tickets in order to have that cost covered. The musicians are donating their time, of course, and so I think that we're doing pretty well. Although... I don't know if we'll be able to sell enough tickets to make it possible for us to pay for the supplies it would take to make a raised platform."

"People might donate it." Olivia tapped her chin.

"That's true. I think maybe I'll go around and ask some of the business owners if they might be interested in chipping in towards it, and then... I don't know if we can make a sign or something announcing that they supported it, just to give their business a little lift and to give them a little more incentive to donate?"

"I bet we could. I could actually come up with something," Olivia said thoughtfully. Making candles was her crafty outlet, but before she did candles full-time, she fiddled around with some other crafty things. She could certainly make a sign with some names on it. "I know calligraphy, and I might need a little bit of help getting a stake or something to attach the sign to, but I can definitely make the sign."

"All right then. That sounds perfect. I'll let you know how my fundraising efforts go," Grace said, winking as she stood and looked around the room.

A few families played some board games together, while several others sat in a big circle on the floor chatting. A bunch of older ladies sat in chairs along the edge of the wall, and Olivia knew that those ladies had been matchmaking all day.

Thankfully, she had been left out of that, since they had been focusing on the younger kids, teens and college age. She supposed that someone her age wasn't a huge magnet for matchmakers. After all, she was past the stage where she had stars in her eyes about romance, or would feel like she was going head over heels for anyone.

As soon as she thought that, Mark's face crossed her mind.

A little shiver went down her backbone, and she wondered if maybe she really wasn't too old to feel like a teenager again.

She didn't want to. She didn't have room for that in her life. She was too busy trying to survive, to raise her children, to be the best mom that she could be, and to give back to the community that had given to her so generously.

But Mark was giving back to that same community, and they seemed to work pretty well together. They had a lot of things in common, although they didn't have to have everything in common. She always thought that it was the differences between Cam and her that really made their relationship interesting. He was able to teach her things, and she taught him a few things too. Although, they'd spent so much time apart with him being deployed that she felt like they'd lost that a little bit.

It wasn't good to have too much space between a couple. Definitely. Maybe that was common sense, but in hindsight, she and Cam definitely had drifted apart. Not that it mattered anymore. She just wanted to be sure that whoever she was with, she made time for them. If she ever had a relationship again, she wanted to be with someone who would make time for her, and she wanted to be sure that she did the same. After all, once the children were gone, she would have to look at that person across the supper table every night, without the buffer of kids between them. They needed to actually like each other.

Her eyes drifted across the room, and she saw Mark working with Isadora and the children.

They made a nice couple, and they too worked well together.

Despite herself, she watched them for a little bit longer, trying to quell whatever ugly feeling was rising up in her.

Was that jealousy?

Her throat clenched as Isadora laughed at something Mark had said.

Yeah. It must be jealousy. Because while the logical part of her could say that they looked good together, there was a part of her that wanted to go over there and interrupt, to break it up, to get them apart.

But she didn't give into that side of her personality. Isadora would actually be perfect for Mark. She would be a wonderful pastor's wife, she was great with kids, and already taught a Sunday school class.

She could integrate well into the church, and Mark seemed fond of her.

She shook the thought out of her head and turned away, trying to figure out what she was doing before she was distracted by Mark and Isadora.

She managed to bury herself in work, and only glanced up once in a while to make sure her twins were behaving, but otherwise ignoring Mark and Isadora.

It surprised her when Mark showed up at her shoulder.

"Grace told me to come see you about where I should stand for the concert. She said you had a drawing already."

He startled her, and she tried to catch her breath unobtrusively before she nodded. "Yes. I do. I set it down over here." She pointed to a little stand sitting behind the table where they served the soup.

It was going to be ready in just a few minutes, and Marjorie McBride had already asked her to finish up what she was doing so she could make her way over to the serving table.

"If you're busy, you don't have to do it right now."

"Oh, it's not a problem. I was heading this way anyway," she said.

"Your boys are managing somehow to charm everyone in the room. Look at them now," Mark said, nodding over toward where Aiden and Ethan were speaking with the group of old ladies who had parked their chairs together and were pretending to knit but were actually matchmaking.

"They just love people. Especially Aiden."

"Isadora and I were saying how cute they were. And her kids just seem to... we had to remind her kids several times not to play favorites. Those boys are something else."

Like any normal parent, it warmed Olivia's heart and soul to hear someone complimenting her children.

Even though she tried hard to ignore the fact that Mark was basically praising Isadora as well. And her children.

"I worry so much that I'm ruining them, you know?"

"Weren't you the one that was telling me earlier today that God isn't giving us anything that He isn't going to help us handle? That we have everything we need for the job that He's put in front of us?"

She laughed and shook her head. "You are so right. I don't know why I don't apply that to my situation. I feel like the boys don't have a father and therefore they have a handicap in life. You know?"

"I do believe that it's important for a child to grow up in a two-parent home. That's the way God intended it, and that's the way children thrive. There is no doubt about that. But it's true that God promises to be with you always, and to help you. And it's also true that He has a plan for your life, and for theirs. And if His plan had been for their dad to survive, he would have."

His voice held compassion and kindness, and she knew he was saying it in the sweetest and most loving way possible. He wasn't trying to rub in her face that her husband had died.

"I'm sorry to bring up what have to be painful memories," he said.

"No. It's not a problem. It's been long enough ago that I still get a twinge, but it's mostly because of my sadness for the boys. Never knowing their father, never getting to have any memories with him at all. That type of thing. For me... I guess I wish that I would've had a marriage where I celebrated a fiftieth anniversary. But... I guess that wasn't what God had for me."

"No. It's sometimes one of the hardest things to accept, that what we want isn't what God wants for us. That's tough."

"Boy. I agree with you completely."

They'd made it to the little stand, and she picked the paper up.

"I was thinking about you being right here. Grace and I were just talking about this earlier, and if we have the money, we're going to see if we can have a raised platform. Which I think will make the candlelight more visible to everyone. The arrangement of the musicians won't be quite as important, but we've tried to do it so that the most angles have good views. We have you sitting in a chair over here, and then, when it's time for you to stand up and speak, you'll move to here."

Mark nodded, looking like he approved of her plan.

"That's brilliant. I love that you really thought this out and have chosen the absolute best way to arrange things. I'm impressed." He looked at her, his eyes twinkling, and for a few moments, it was as though everyone in the large room faded away, and it was just Mark and her in the world together.

She'd never experienced that before, where it felt like they were the only two in the world. Even with Cam.

She didn't know how long the moment would've lasted, but Marjorie McBride spoke, and the spell was broken.

"I'm so glad you're here. I've got the boys carrying your soup out, and I do believe everyone is starving. And that bread smells amazing."

If Marjorie noticed there was anything amiss, she didn't say, and Olivia certainly didn't bring attention to it.

Instead, she cleared her throat, which suddenly felt constricted, and willed her mouth to make saliva, since it was suddenly powder dry.

"I'll leave you to your duties. Thank you for showing me. That's a brilliant arrangement." Pastor Mark pointed at the paper, and then nodded at her and walked away.

As had become the custom, he would pray before the meal, and then he would wait until everyone else had been served before he got his own food. Olivia had noticed that he had done that with every meal that they served.

It was impressive, and in her opinion, it showed true leadership. Where the leader made sure that everyone following him was nourished before he nourished himself.

It flew in the face of what modern society often told people, that you've got to take care of yourself before you can take care of anyone else, and it harkened back to what she always heard about George Washington, making sure his men ate before he did. It was a biblical principle, with Jesus washing the disciples' feet and caring for others before he cared for himself.

Mark definitely lived a life that pointed people to Jesus. To her, that was impressive.

Chapter Seventeen

"$\mathcal{I}$ have a buddy at the power company, and he said that Mistletoe Meadows is next on the list. He said power could be on to select homes even before midnight tonight."

Mark nodded as Ben spoke low into his ear.

Most of the families had retreated to their corners and were reading stories, singing songs, and otherwise getting their children calmed down and ready for bed.

The older ladies had lain down on their cots, although they must still have had their hearing aids in, because they spoke low.

Mark observed the interactions, making sure teenagers stayed with their families, and didn't go wandering around having some clandestine meeting. He didn't want the church's reputation to be one where promiscuity abounded, not even a little bit.

"Thanks for the report. We had a pretty good day, but I know people are getting restless, and also concerned about the lack of work. I truly hope some folks can start going back to their homes tomorrow."

"I think they should be. The snow stopped earlier this evening, although our road isn't plowed. It's probably going to take some heavy equipment to move that much snow. From what I understand, the interstate is okay, though."

"The trucks were able to keep that clean?"

"That's where they had to focus all of their resources. But they'll start opening up the side roads soon. Down below, once you get out of the mountains, they didn't get nearly as much snow, so we should be seeing trucks tonight, overnight, or tomorrow morning, I would think."

"Well, that's good news. I don't think I'll say anything to anyone, though, because I don't want to get their hopes up."

"No. I just wanted to let you know what I knew, so that we were on the same page, with the same timeline in mind."

"All right, I appreciate it."

"How's the food holding out?"

"We've got plenty. Although, if Marjorie McBride hadn't come bearing loads and loads of food, we might've been out by now. Thankfully, we had a couple of farmers in the area donate some meat as well."

"It's always good to have some friends that can feed you," Ben laughed.

"I never realized just how true that could be," Mark said.

They grinned, as Ben moved away, finding his wife, who was talking to one of the older ladies who had been a little short of breath.

Mark had been keeping an eye on that situation. He didn't think it was anything serious, but he also wanted to be sure that they were on top of things. If they had to figure out how to get someone to the hospital, they were going to do it.

As his eyes scanned over the room, they caught for a moment on Olivia, as she snuggled with her boys, one on either side of her. She had a book in her lap, and they leaned against her as she read it to them quietly. He couldn't pick her voice out of the crowd, but he didn't need to. Just looking at her was enough.

He'd been aware of her presence all day—where she was, what she was doing—and had found himself wanting to go over and talk to her more than once, even though he didn't really have anything to say. He just wanted to check in on her, make sure she was okay, chat about the weather or something else that didn't mean anything, just to have that connection with her.

He knew what that meant, although he hadn't felt it before. It meant that the attraction he felt was getting stronger.

Lord, should I pursue this? Could you tell me for sure if I should?

He knew that God did not work that way. After all, God gave him the principles in the Bible, and if he lived his life according to those, he would probably remain in God's will. Sometimes there just wasn't a right or wrong answer.

But the idea of striking up a romantic relationship could have huge implications throughout the entire community, and he didn't want to mess it up.

After all, a bad breakup could be painful for both of them, and could also jeopardize his position in the church. He didn't want to be known as the man who went from relationship to relationship to relationship, with none of them working out. He wanted to enter a relationship with the idea that they were building something solid and long-term.

Was he really thinking about a relationship with Olivia?

Maybe that was moving a little too fast. Maybe he should have given in to his urges and talked with her a little bit more today. He definitely wanted to spend more time with her. He enjoyed playing with her boys and getting to know them. Although, when he overheard one of them telling a friend that Pastor Mark could be their dad, it hadn't scared him the way he thought it should. On the contrary, he thought, *Yeah. I could.*

Oddly, he had been talking to Olivia about that very thing, the boys needing a dad. And he had been assuring her that God would provide if they actually needed it.

How ironic, if God had been intending to provide him as the father all along.

He was definitely getting the cart ahead of the horse. For now, he needed to just relax and let things work. Let God work things the way He wanted to.

Chapter Eighteen

"Thank you so much for staying here." Pastor Mark shook Ralph Jones's hand as the man harrumphed.

"It's me that should be thanking you. You saved my wife and me an awful lot of cold nights. The last time we lost power, we were huddled under blankets together to stay warm, and by the time the power came back on, I wasn't completely sure whether she was more ready to kill me, or I was more ready to kill her," he said, glancing down fondly at his wife, who looked up at him, shaking her head.

"That's quite a story," was all she said.

Mark laughed, although inside he wondered what it would be like to have someone to snuggle with under the blankets and keep warm. He hardly thought he'd be interested in killing her. It might not be something that he'd choose to do on a normal day, but he could think of ways to pass the time that would make snuggling under the blankets not unpleasant.

But he laughed good-naturedly and closed the door behind the last guest to leave.

After three full nights and two full days—electricity for pretty much all the surrounding areas had come back on. Except for the opposite side of the street in Mistletoe Meadows.

He looked at the dark candle shop. Still no lights there.

"Well, you're down to just us. I'm sorry to be a bother." Olivia walked up to him, her hands shoved in her pockets, her mouth turned down.

Her boys played happily around the large activity room. With all the cots put away and the sleeping bags rolled up, they had the entire place to themselves. Plus, since they were no longer trying to conserve electricity so that the generator wouldn't run out of fuel, but instead they now had electricity and the lights were on, they were taking advantage of their newfound spacious play area.

"You're not inconveniencing me in any way. In fact, I was thinking that if you don't mind, I'll put you guys up in my guestroom so we can all enjoy the luxuries of having hot showers nearby, and a kitchen as well."

"Oh my goodness. I couldn't possibly—"

"It would actually be more convenient for me to have you there than here." He couldn't really articulate why that was. But it was true. Having them in his house would make it easier for him to keep an eye on them, and serve them the way he wanted to. Plus, he wanted to do the very best that he could for Olivia.

"Are you sure?" she asked, biting her lip and looking like she was ready to grab her kids and run back to the cold and dark candle shop.

"I insist. Please, let me do this."

"All right. But only if you let me help."

"I'll tell you what, I'll let you help by rolling up your sleeping bags and tidying up your area. I'll go grab sheets and blankets and make up the beds in the spare rooms."

She seemed reluctant, but she nodded her head and said, "All right."

He hummed to himself as he walked back through his house, enjoying the fact that every time he turned on the switch, there was light. What a tiny thing to take for granted, but what a huge thing when one didn't have it.

Thank you, Lord, for electricity. Thank you that the entire town seemed to get along, and that we had some new converts, and people who decided to start coming back to church. That more than made everything worthwhile, although he would've done it without that, just because he knew it was what God wanted.

It was true—the idea of having more people in church, and that several people had gotten saved because of the gospel message that had been presented each evening as they did their evening Bible study and prayer time, had more than made up for any kind of inconvenience. Although, he really didn't consider it an inconvenience. It was just an opportunity to serve. To give back to God who had given so much to him.

He was just finishing putting the blanket on the twins' bed when Olivia stepped into the doorway.

"Is there anything I can do to help?"

"Not a thing. If you want to go ahead and give the twins a bath, get them ready for bed, you're certainly welcome to do that. I'm going to go over and make up the bed in your room."

"Oh, you don't have to do that. I know how to make a bed."

"I want to. I was just thinking that I appreciate the opportunity that God has given me to serve others, and I feel like it's the least I can do for everything that he's done for me. Sometimes I forget how blessed I am."

Her brows went up a bit, as though she were surprised that he was articulating it like that. But then she nodded, as though she understood the truth in his words.

"Thank you. Thank you for your service, but also thank you for the reminder. Sometimes I resent all the work I have to do to keep a roof over our heads, and to take care of the boys by myself. But... you're right. Serving them is like serving God, and I should be grateful for the opportunity to give back."

She didn't stand in the doorway, but disappeared once more.

He smiled at her words. Some people would argue with him and continue to be disgruntled. It showed what a servant's heart and what a malleable personality Olivia had that instead of being upset, she looked at herself and saw there were things she could improve.

Mark had worked with people long enough to know that even Christians could get set in their ways and refuse to see that they could become better.

He made the bed that she would be sleeping in, listening to the sounds of the boys splashing in the tub coming down the hall. Was this what it would be like if they had children of their own? If he had a family of his own?

He wouldn't mind having the laughter and the fun, but he knew that it would be a lot of work. But like he told Olivia, he didn't mind the work. As long as he had the right mindset, that serving others was a small way that he could give back to the Lord for everything that God had done for him.

He had found that a lot of times his contentment had more to do with his mindset than with his circumstances. He supposed that's why God commanded Christians in Philippians to focus on what was good and right and true and beautiful. Because when a person did that, when they were thankful and looked at Jesus rather than the circumstances around them or the people around them, they had a tendency to be less depressed and more joyful.

God had the recipe. It was too bad that so many Christians refused to follow it. It was almost like they didn't believe that God knew what he was talking about. But Mark could tell from experience that it was true. And it worked.

"We want Pastor Mark to pray with us like he did when everybody was there," Aiden said, as Olivia wrapped the towel around Ethan, and both of the boys ran to their room. "Aren't you coming?"

Pastor Mark chuckled to himself. He highly doubted the boys wanted a Bible lesson. It was more likely that they just wanted the company and to prolong bedtime. But, if they were gonna ask for it, he certainly wasn't going to turn down the opportunity.

"You don't have to," Olivia said softly as she passed him in the hall.

"I'm a pastor. This is my calling. I'm not going to turn down the opportunity to preach the Bible to someone, even if it is a four-year-old."

She half rolled her eyes and continued to walk down the hall.

He loved that she laughed easily, despite the fact that she had so much on her shoulders. He also loved that she took such great care of her boys, but also was concerned about others. All the while, she continued to work, getting orders and trying to make sure that they would have money coming in.

He couldn't imagine having the responsibility for two little lives all on his own shoulders.

He grabbed his Bible, and then walked back to the boys' room, where Olivia sat at the foot of the bed, talking to the kids about what they were all thankful for.

He stood in the doorway, listening, as the boys listed people to play with, toys, Pastor Mark—which made him smile—and all the fun that they'd had over the last few days.

In no way did they insinuate that they were worried or afraid or upset about not being in their house at all. In fact, to hear them talk, they were ready to continue to live a nomadic lifestyle.

He thought about how the Bible told Christians that they were to be as little children. Not a thought of worry in their minds, and he wished that he was that good at not being concerned about anything, but being happy at the change of routine and the excitement that a snowstorm and a power outage could bring into his life.

"Pastor Mark! Are you coming in?" Aiden asked eagerly.

Ethan looked at him with bright eyes as he lay under the covers that were pulled up to his chin.

"If it's okay with your mom," he said easily.

Olivia shifted, nodding and smiling a welcome.

He walked in, chatting easily with the boys as he opened his Bible and read the story of Jesus talking about allowing the little children to come unto him. Then he spoke a few words about how God loved children, and he cared about them, even to the point where he would spend time with children rather than adults. He told the boys that Jesus was always listening, and they could say anything to him. Elementary principles, but principles that adults sometimes forgot. Or sometimes didn't feel, so then they didn't believe were real. But just because someone didn't feel something didn't make it not true. It just made their feelings wrong.

Then the boys bowed their heads, and each of them prayed. Aiden went first, as he usually did, taking the lead, and thanking God for many of the things that he'd already talked to his mom about, and then asking God to make the lights in their house come back on so that their mom could make candles for the church.

That made Pastor Mark smile as he listened, and then Aiden said amen, and Ethan began to pray.

He said a lot of the same things that his brother had, which was a pattern that Mark had noticed. Ethan tended to follow Aiden wherever he went. But then Ethan said something that made Mark's heart stutter to a stop.

"And God, please let Pastor Mark be our dad. So we can live here, and Pastor Mark can take care of Mom, and we could be a family."

Mark didn't listen to anything else the kid said. He was way too aware of the woman beside him, and the fact that God really heard children's prayers. Because they were much less encumbered than adults were.

Of course, he didn't mind that prayer. The idea of being married to Olivia was not onerous, and in fact, as he considered the idea, he realized it was something that he had been hoping for deep down, even if he wasn't admitting it to himself.

But what did Olivia think?

It seemed like a big step to ask her, and while he didn't know a whole lot about women, he knew that a lot of times it took them a little bit longer to make up their mind. Especially when, like Olivia, they had a lot on their shoulders, because they had a tendency to think in terms of the people around them far more than what men did. Mark considered that to be biblical thinking, although he knew the world would criticize someone who considered what other people thought before they made a decision that concerned themselves. It was just one of the ways that the world preached selfishness and elevated it to something that people should aspire to, instead of recognizing it as what human nature naturally did and was not the way a person should live.

Even Christian counselors got it wrong. He'd lost track of the number of times he'd heard or read a so-called Christian say that a person had to take care of themselves first before they could help anyone else. It was such a lie. So not found in the Bible, not even a little bit. A lot of times they would say, "But Jesus went off by himself to pray." And that was true, but typically Jesus went off by himself to pray after he ministered to a great number of people, doing far more than modern Americans could ever dream of. And not that going off by oneself and digging into the Bible and being alone with God was a bad thing. It certainly wasn't. But when modern Americans were told to take care of themselves first, it typically wasn't for them to go off by themselves to pray and read the Bible and be alone with God. It was more likely for them to go get a manicure and turn down people who were asking for help, because they didn't feel like helping or expending that much energy on someone else. But Jesus gave everything for the people around him, holding nothing back.

"Amen," Olivia said softly, and Mark realized that Ethan's prayer was over too.

"All right, boys, I'll see you two turkeys in the morning. Thanks for being great kids today."

He grinned at both of them, kissing their foreheads before he stood and nodded at Olivia, barely meeting her eyes before he walked softly out of the room.

It would be awkward to talk to her again, although perhaps he didn't have to allow it to be so. He could just go on like it wasn't a big deal. Because it wasn't. Kids wanted one thing one minute, and the next minute, they wanted something completely different. So what if Ethan had prayed that Mark would be his dad? And so what if he wasn't against it?

Chapter Nineteen

At five o'clock the next morning, Olivia was out of bed, in the kitchen making coffee.

It did not surprise her at all to hear Mark moving back the hall, and to see him appear in the kitchen.

"Good morning," she said softly.

"Good morning. Did you sleep well?"

He saw that she was making coffee, and he grinned as she poured a cup of straight black and handed it to him.

"I did. Like a baby." She didn't really understand that saying. Her babies hadn't slept all night for at least four months. But he knew what she meant and nodded.

"I'm glad to hear it."

Thankfully, things weren't strained between them this morning as they had been last night after Ethan had prayed that Mark would be his dad and they could be a family together. Olivia had wanted to sink through the floor. It felt like he had gone on and on and on talking about how he wanted a dad and he wanted Mark to be it and he wanted Mark to be part of their family and all of that. And Olivia wanted to lean over to Pastor Mark and say that she had not said anything about that and had not put that idea in his head at all.

But she didn't want to interrupt his prayer, and she also didn't want to draw more attention to it than it needed to be. Maybe Mark wasn't even paying attention to his prayer. After all, he was praying to God, not Mark.

Maybe Mark was thinking about the coming sermon, what he was going to talk about for Christmas.

She had no idea.

Still, it had been a little awkward when they met in the hall and she'd thanked him for his hospitality and told him she was taking a shower and then going to bed.

He seemed like he wanted to talk about something else, but she just wanted to escape.

But that was last night. Now, they both sat down at the kitchen table with their Bibles open, and an hour slipped by before she even knew it. There was companionable silence, and it felt good and right to have Mark beside her, as he talked to the Lord, just as she did.

She actually had a few things she was studying that she wouldn't have minded talking to him about, but she didn't want to bother him and didn't know how he felt about that. Although, she kind of thought he wouldn't mind, considering that the night before he had explained that anytime he had a chance to talk about the Bible with someone, he eagerly did.

She had just opened her mouth to ask what he thought about a particular passage when his phone buzzed.

He looked over at it, picking it up and reading a text.

"That's John at the power company. He said that he thought the lights on the other side of the road might be on later today, possibly this afternoon. They think they've found the problem, but they need another truck, and everyone has been dispatched somewhere."

"Oh. That would be wonderful. I've been trying not to think about all the candles I have to make."

He grinned. "We have to make. Remember? I said I would help you."

"I do remember. But I also know that this is your busy time of year, and I don't expect you to help me if you just can't."

"You don't expect me to keep my word? Tell me you have higher standards for me than that."

"Well, when you put it that way, I guess I do expect you to help me."

He smiled at her, and he seemed totally at ease, which enabled her to feel like that as well.

"Well, that's good. It makes me feel better that we won't be inconveniencing you any longer, even though I know you said we weren't," she said, adding that last part when he put a hand up and opened his mouth as though he were going to contradict her. She couldn't imagine that having people in his house, including two four-year-olds, wasn't an inconvenience at some level.

"I just really loved having the laughter and the splashing and the conversation and just everything about last night," he said.

That made her close her mouth and look down at her Bible on the table. Everything? Even when Ethan had prayed that Mark would be his dad?

She just did not have the nerve to ask that, and so she didn't say anything.

"Olivia, I am—" His phone rang, and she looked up, saw the frustration on his face, and thought for a second that maybe he wasn't going to answer.

"I'm sorry, I probably should get this. Unless you had something else you wanted to say?" he asked, and she thought maybe there was hope in his voice. Was he wanting her to bring that subject up?

There was no way. She wasn't going to say a word about that if she could get away with not. Although... what would it hurt? They could just talk about it and see how they felt.

Maybe he was okay with that idea. And honestly, she was busy being embarrassed about it, mostly because she was okay with that idea. But she didn't want him to know, especially if he was looking for someone who was super spiritual and well respected in the community to be his wife. After all, that was hardly her.

She felt like she was hanging onto her spirituality by a thread. The rift with her parents made her feel guilty, and she had been withdrawing from the community more than she realized. Being shut up with everyone in the activity room made her see that she had been keeping herself from accepting help, and also from giving it. She just had her head down, focused on all the things that she needed to do in order to function. But that wasn't the kind of life she wanted to live.

"No. You go ahead and get it," she said, and he looked at her for another moment before he nodded, and then swiped.

She stood up, closing her Bible and putting it on the counter, before deciding that she might as well make some bread. Mark seemed to really like it, and she might as well make herself useful.

She hummed as he carried on a conversation in low tones while still seated at the table. And she moved around the kitchen, getting the ingredients out that she needed, and then running to the kitchen in the activity center in order to get yeast, which unsurprisingly, he didn't have.

By the time she got back and had the bread in a greased bowl to rise, Ethan came out, rubbing his eyes and looking sleepy.

It was about time for both of them to get up, and she bent down, picking him up and squeezing him to her. She loved this time of day when her kids were all cuddly from sleep, and before their hyper energy kicked in and they didn't want to be still for two seconds to get a hug from their mom.

"Are you hungry?" she asked, looking at the bacon and eggs that she'd brought over from the activity center that had been left over. People had donated them to help feed the people the church was housing, and she figured that meant she could go ahead and use them, since the church was still technically housing her.

"I am! Are you making breakfast?"

"I sure am, buddy. Why don't you grab a chair, and you can help me crack some eggs."

She set Aiden down, and then cautioned him, "Pastor Mark is on the phone, so you need to be quiet, okay?"

He nodded, used to such a command, because she'd had no choice but to conduct business around her children, and they knew that occasionally she needed to be on the phone and they needed to be quiet. They actually did a pretty good job with that, although they were children, not perfect.

"I hope it's okay with you if I go out. There are a few people that need me to check on them."

She turned around quickly, not realizing that Mark had ended his phone call.

"Of course not. I wouldn't want to keep you from doing your job."

He looked at her as though he wanted to say something else, was thinking about something, but he just shook his head.

"Please make yourself at home. Use whatever you need to, help yourself to anything. There's nothing you can do that will hurt anything."

"Thank you. I have a few ideas that might involve homemade bread, if you don't mind."

"Of course I'm not going to mind anything that you cook, and who in the world would fuss about homemade bread?" He grinned. "I'll be looking forward to it."

There was something about his smile that made her stomach curl. That, and the fact that he was looking forward to eating with her.

"I'm serious. Help yourself to anything." He glanced over his shoulder. "And don't worry about the boys. There's nothing they can hurt."

"I might want to go over and check out my shop and apartment."

"If you don't mind waiting, I'll do it with you. Even if we do it after we put the boys to bed." He looked over his shoulder. "By then the lights might be on, and I can get started on fulfilling my promise of helping you."

She grinned, but then her brows drew down. "I don't want to take you from your other duties."

"You are just as important as anyone else in my flock." He opened his mouth as though to say more, but then closed it. "And I promised I would help you. I like to keep my promises if at all possible. I feel like that's important."

She jerked her head in a nod. Of course it was important. Especially for a pastor, but for anyone who claimed to be a Christian, they needed to do what they said they were going to do.

"All right. Well, let me know when you're getting back. I'll make sure there's hot food for you."

"Oh boy. You're going to spoil me."

"Sounds like it's about time someone did," she said, although she turned back to the stove and did not watch for his reaction. Maybe she shouldn't have said it, but she was getting the impression that he gave all of himself for anyone who needed it, and there was no one here to look after him. To make sure he was eating and taking care of himself, and being there to take care of him.

"Olivia?"

"Yes?"

"Thank you."

Her hands stilled on the rag as she wiped the counter, but then she looked over her shoulder. "Of course. Like I said, someone needs to."

Chapter Twenty

Mark couldn't wait to get home. The idea of freshly baked, warm bread, and something yummy and hot in his stomach made him anxious to leave the last three houses he visited. But Mrs. Tucker had made some care packages, and she wanted him to deliver them, and then he'd ended up helping to shovel Miss Crosby's mailbox out. She didn't drive a car anymore, but it was important to her to be able to get to her paper and her mail deliveries, although he wasn't even sure the mail was going to be delivered today. As the day wore on, more and more of the roads were cleared, but there were still folks who were without power and could not get out of their driveway.

As far as he could determine, he'd contacted everyone who was a member of the congregation, and others who were not members but who attended occasionally. Everyone seemed to be okay, and he had started stopping at random houses that didn't look like they had any activity outside.

He found two older couples who had needed his help, and several young couples who didn't need his help but appreciated his attention. One of those asked about services, and he was pretty sure he would be seeing them over the Christmas season.

A snowstorm was a great time for a pastor to get out and try to go above and beyond, not for himself or his own glory, but for Jesus.

Still, the idea of Olivia at home, cooking and baking bread, and the idea that there would be company and coziness in his home, made him eager to return.

He hoped she didn't decide that she needed to go home. Although, he couldn't bring himself to hope that her electricity was not back on. After all, he knew she had a lot of work to do, and she was probably eager to get back to her home.

As eager as he was for her to stay.

Thankfully, the scent of warm, fresh-baked bread drifted out as he opened the door and stepped in.

Aiden and Ethan jumped up from their toys and ran to him, hugging him like they'd known him for all of their lives, instead of just for the last few weeks.

"Mommy said we could eat when you get home!" Ethan said, bursting the bubble that had formed around Mark, thinking that they liked him for him. He laughed, because they were excited to see him because they were going to get food.

But maybe they liked him a little, he thought, as they grabbed a hold of his hands and chattered about their day. Ethan was obviously feeling more comfortable with him, since he chatted almost as much as his brother did.

"Where's your mother?" he asked, as he walked through the living room and into the kitchen.

"I'm right here. And you have perfect timing. I'm just taking the bread out of the oven."

"Wow. That really is perfect timing."

"I made a couple of loaves earlier today and put those in the freezer for you. You can get those out and heat those up. It won't be quite as good as freshly baked, but it'll be close."

She had made bread and frozen it for him? He loved that she was industrious, keeping herself occupied all day.

"I've gotten a text from my buddy at the electric company. He said he thought your power would be on this evening sometime before midnight."

"That's great," she said, although maybe she didn't look quite as excited as she could have that she could be going back to her place tomorrow.

Or maybe he was just reading more into it than he should. After all, he wanted her to want to stay.

Maybe they could talk tonight.

"Is there something I can do to help with supper? The boys informed me that we were eating when I got home, so I assume that there's something almost ready."

"You could just sit down and take it easy. I'll have it on the table here in about five minutes."

"Or... it sounds like you've been as busy as I have today, and I would like to help you if there's something I can do."

As tempting as it might be to sit down and kick back, he didn't want her doing all the work. Especially since it was obvious that she had worked all day as well.

"All right. I just needed to chop these vegetables for a salad, and cut the bread."

He grabbed the knife and began to cut the tomatoes she had pointed out.

"How was your day?" he asked, feeling very domestic. Was this what it would be like to come home to a wife? To Olivia?

He didn't even stop himself from thinking that, because he kind of felt like maybe God had orchestrated this, and he was resisting unnecessarily. Although, he certainly couldn't force Olivia to do anything she didn't want to, nor did he want to do that. He wanted Olivia to want him for him.

"Well, you said I should make myself at home, so I went ahead and got all the perishable items that were left in the church kitchen and brought them over here. That's how I was able to make the vegetable soup. And I made a little dessert as well with the leftover dairy stuff."

"Wow. Dessert? That sounds awesome."

"Someone has a sweet tooth?" she asked, giving him a calculating look.

"Guilty," he said, raising his hand.

They laughed together. "Anyway, I cleaned the kitchen over there and organized it. Nothing that's going to make any of the ladies upset, I don't think anyway. But I just made sure everything was neatly put away and ready for the next time."

"I don't know if I want there to be a next time. People are still digging out from this one."

"How was your day?" she asked. "Are there lots of people still snowed in?"

"There are a few. Especially people with longer driveways. It's a lot to shovel. I did a little shoveling myself, met a few new people, one couple that I'm pretty sure we're going to see in church. If not this Sunday, sometime around Christmas."

"That's great! Who would've thought that God could use... I guess it shouldn't surprise us that God could use a snowstorm to bring people to him."

"No. But somehow the way he works always does have a tendency to... if not surprise me, amaze me."

"Same. I love that He uses things that no one else thinks He could."

"His creativity is awesome."

He put the tomatoes on the lettuce she had sitting out, and then began to chop the carrots.

"Aiden, please set the silverware on the table at each place. Ethan, fold a napkin and set it beside each plate."

Mark waited until the boys did her bidding.

"You do an excellent job with them."

"They love you. They couldn't wait for you to come home."

"I would be flattered, except I'm pretty sure they couldn't wait for me to get home because they were going to eat when I got here. They're typical boys, and had their stomachs totally in mind."

She laughed, as he had intended, and her laugh made him warm all the way to the soles of his feet and back.

"Well, that part is true. I did tell them that we weren't eating until you got home. But they talked about you all day. And they truly do adore you."

He loved that—that her children loved him just as much as he loved them.

"They're great kids. I don't want to play favorites, because as a pastor I'm pretty sure I'm supposed to be impartial, but they were definitely my favorite children of all the kids that were there these last few days. They just have such sweet personalities about them. And maybe it's because there's two of them, and they play off of each other, but they just have a heart for people, even at this young age."

"You know, Mrs. Tucker has watched them an awful lot, and I know that she has really taught them about not being selfish, and sharing and loving other people. I'm afraid that I can't take any credit for that."

"I'd say you certainly can. After all, whatever they've been learning at home has probably been reinforced by Mrs. Tucker. Plus, they just have those natural abilities that sometimes you see early in people."

"I hope you're right. I guess that's one of my biggest fears. That somehow I'll screw my kids up irreparably and that it'll be all my fault. You know?"

"I totally get it. But I think that's what we talked about a little bit before. Just having faith that God's going to work things out. That whatever He's planned and ordained is exactly right. After all, there was nothing you did wrong to have those boys lose their father."

"No. And I understand that, but maybe I'm missing something. Maybe He had another father lined up for them, and I was just too focused on my work and on trying to keep my head above water to even pay any attention. Maybe I've missed out on things that I should've been doing, or maybe I did things that I shouldn't—"

He put a hand up. She closed her mouth abruptly. "And you just have to pray and ask God to help you follow Him. And then, keep an eye on and an ear out, but at the same time, you can't sweat it. If God wants you to do it, it's not like He's going to tuck a clue in the far corner of the back forty, and you're going to dig a fifteen foot hole and use a microscope in order to find it. He's not going to make it that hard. He wants you to succeed. He's on your side. Or I guess I should say we're on His side, and He loves us. Just like a father isn't going to make his child's life miserable on purpose. A father is going to help him in every way possible. At least if he's a good dad."

"Do you see a lot of families that have parents that aren't good?" she asked, seeming to read his mind.

"I do. But that's not the point, is it? The point is, God wants you to succeed. And if you want to do what God wants you to do, I don't think that God is going to make it hard for you to figure out what that is. I just don't."

"Sometimes it seems like it's hard."

"Do you think we make it harder than what it needs to be?"

"I think I do sometimes. But other times, it's just hard to know, you know? Like... maybe I should've sold the shop and done something else to support them. Or maybe I should be more actively looking for a husband to be a dad. I just..." She bit her lip. "I don't want to make the same mistake again."

"Mistake?"

She pressed her lips together, and then looked over her shoulder.

"My parents didn't think that I should've married Cam. Maybe they were right."

"Is the food almost ready?"

Aiden effectively interrupted their conversation, just as Mark was hanging on her every word. What mistake had she made with Cam? Other than her parents not approving. He knew that she was estranged from her parents. Was that why?

He had a lot of things he wanted to talk to her about, but it couldn't be when the children were around and listening. Their conversation had been low enough, and the twins had been yammering between themselves, so he hadn't been worried about them hearing, but that was definitely not a conversation that would be meant for little ears.

Lord, if we're supposed to talk about this, please present the opportunity again.

Chapter Twenty-One

"I think they're asleep," Olivia said, as she backed away from the twins' door. It was cracked just a bit, and she could see them snuggled under the blankets, sleeping peacefully.

"All right. It's obvious that your side of the street is still dark, but I've got flashlights."

Mark held out a light for her, and she thanked him as she took it.

"Have you heard any updates?" Honestly, being with Mark in his house, spending the evening with him and the boys had felt like family. She really wouldn't mind staying, which made her feel like she really needed to go.

"No. I haven't heard anything."

"All right," she said, hating that she felt relief. Like she would have another night and morning in the kitchen with Mark, making coffee, laughing together, reading their Bibles and having devotions at the table as the sun came up.

She couldn't think of anything she would rather do. She'd never felt so comfortable with someone, and so... cared for without being smothered.

After she got her coat on and wrapped her scarf around her neck, tucking the edges into her coat, he opened the door for her, and they walked out onto the sidewalk.

"It looks so odd, with one side of the street being all lit up."

She had to agree. "I've never seen the town quite like this."

"I don't know that this is normal, but it seems to be a fluke of the storm."

As they strolled, snow flurries fell softly, not enough to amount to anything, just enough to make it feel cozy.

But as she stepped out to cross the mostly deserted street, lights blinked on the other side, and then came on.

"Look! Perfect timing." Mark smiled, and then looked at her.

She knew she was supposed to be happy, but she was watching him. Was he happy to finally get the rest of the people out of his house? It felt like it, but there was definitely something that looked like disappointment on his face. Probably the same look that was on hers.

"Well, that's great. We can see how everything fared, now that the lights are on," she said. God's timing was perfect, she supposed. And if she wasn't supposed to stay with Mark, then that was the way it was.

She pulled the key out of her pocket, and Mark glanced at her, then held his hand out for it.

It made her feel like he was taking care of her again. Unlocking the door, walking with her while she checked on things, but not pushing in, or making her feel like she couldn't handle it on her own. Just making her feel like he cared and wanted to take care of her. It was a good feeling.

"This will be good news for your candle orders. And for your bottom line."

"Yeah. I've been eager to get started. Part of the reason I stayed so busy today was so that I wasn't thinking about what I needed to do."

"I'll help you. We'll get that done."

She nodded, stepping into the shop as he opened the door for her.

She appreciated him caring and being concerned that her business was profitable. He really didn't need to, and they both knew it, but he did. Although, she had to admit to herself that it wasn't just her. He was like this with everyone. Always going out of his way to do whatever he could to help. Maybe she wasn't as special as she wanted to think she was.

"Well, it doesn't look like any pipes burst, at least not down here," she said as she glanced around, checking the sink in the bathroom and the one out by her workshop.

"You know, I don't hear your furnace running," Mark said thoughtfully.

"Now that you mention it, I don't either." Olivia tilted her head, as though that would help her hear better, but he was right. The furnace was not running.

"If you don't mind, I'll go ahead and go down to the basement and see what I can find."

"I don't mind at all. I'm gonna go upstairs and look around. I shut the water off down there, so would you mind turning it on... or... maybe not. I guess if the furnace isn't running, we better not turn the water back on."

"No. And that showed a lot of foresight on your part, and would be the reason why the pipes aren't leaking."

She made quick work of going upstairs and looking around. The apartment was small, with only two small bedrooms and a living room, dining room, kitchen combo.

Everything looked just fine, and she had packed well, forgetting nothing, so there wasn't anything she needed to pick up. She had drained the toilet as well as the faucets, so no water dripped out at all.

The lights worked just fine, but still, she felt no heat from the registers.

As she walked back downstairs, Mark was coming up from the

basement. She waited until he had gotten to the top and closed the door. She hated going down there. Even though there were lights, it was still dark and creepy, and she always felt like she was going to see some kind of animal huddled back in the corner. She never had, but that didn't make it less scary for her.

"Well?" she asked.

His lips pressed together, and he shook his head. "I tried the relay switch, and a couple of other little tricks I know. I'm not a repairman or a furnace expert by any stretch, and I'll just be honest. I have no idea whether it's something that's fixable or not. But I couldn't get it to work."

"I know nothing about furnaces, and I would have no idea of what to do. Or actually, I wouldn't even be able to find the furnace, I don't think. Unless it says 'furnace' on it."

He laughed, and she supposed it was funny. Although she doubted that anything in the basement had a label on it.

"I guess I'll need to call the furnace repairman, but I'll probably wait until morning. Unless...I don't want to overstay my welcome—"

"You and the boys are welcome to stay as long as you need to. And if that means that you're still in my house this time next Christmas, I'm totally fine with that." He paused for just a moment, and then he said, "The congregation might have some problems with it, though."

"Oh, having a woman living with you?" She nodded. "Yeah. That probably doesn't look very good."

"Giving you a place to stay while you don't have electricity or heat," he added with emphasis on the heat, "is perfectly fine. And you can stay as long as you want to. If anyone says anything, I can find a different place to go."

"No way. I will not allow that to happen. You are not allowed to leave your home while I stay there with my kids."

"Olivia." His voice was soft, and it made her lift her head, meeting his eyes. His hand came out and touched her arm.

She was very aware of her breath, how it kind of stuttered in her lungs with each intake, and how her heart all of a sudden felt like it was running a race.

"Olivia. I don't want to make things weird between us. But you know how we were talking about God's timing, and how He arranges things perfectly?"

She nodded.

"I was thinking that maybe He did that for us. No pressure," he added quickly, as though he wanted to make sure that he wasn't insisting that she needed to do something that she wasn't feeling. She wanted to tell him he didn't need to worry about that. But she kept her mouth closed while he continued. "I find myself drawn to you. Thinking about you when you're not around. When I'm gone, my eyes seem to find you in whatever room we're in, and I want to watch you. I... I don't know exactly what that means, whether you feel anything too. But I want to be careful about my feelings. I think sometimes we get carried away with how we feel, and we run ahead of what God wants for us. But I suppose that's where I started. It feels like God might want something for us. At least that's the way it seems on my end."

She nodded. "I've thought that too. I have the same feelings where I have a tendency to want to watch you. But I would be a terrible choice for a pastor's wife. And I wouldn't want to play around with just dating for dating's sake."

"Same. There's no question that if I'm going to be interested in someone, it's going to lead to marriage, and that is going to happen quickly. I don't want to date for years and years like we can't make up our minds about what God's will is. Or we're going to make a decision quickly that we're not right together. Because dating just for the sake of having someone to date and having it drag on while we're all wishy-washy is not something that I want to have anything to do with."

"Me too." She couldn't believe he was admitting that or saying that. She wasn't sure she'd ever met a man who didn't want to try out the wares, so to speak.

"What does this mean?" she asked, knowing that the part of her that always needed to know where things were going, what was going to happen, was coming out.

He shook his head. "I don't know. I hadn't gotten any further than wanting to check and see if that might be something that you might be interested in."

"I'm definitely interested. But I agree with you that I don't want it to be based on feelings, or at least feelings alone. I want us to... if I'm going to be with someone, it's got to be following God's leading first, and I think that means making sure that we're on the same page. And you didn't address the fact that I would be a terrible pastor's wife."

"I disagree. You're great with people, you're patient with children, and you're good with them. Plus, you're a good cook. You did an excellent job of whatever needed to be done while we were all cooped up together. Plus, sometimes when I've talked to you, I thought to myself that you know the Bible as well or better than I do."

"Knowing it and living it are two different things."

"I don't live it perfectly. I certainly wouldn't expect anyone else to. And God doesn't expect us to. He knows we have a sin nature. Although, that doesn't give us license to sin. It just means that God knows that we're not going to be perfect. Otherwise we wouldn't need Jesus."

"True."

"How about we figure out what we're gonna do with your furnace, then we'll close things up here, turn the lights out, and we'll go over and I'll make a couple of cups of hot chocolate and we can sit down and maybe talk a little bit? Decide if both of us want to go in the same direction?" He smiled and then he said, "And maybe you can laugh a little, because every time you laugh, it just warms me from the inside out. I don't think that I could ever get tired of hearing that sound."

Maybe those weren't the most romantic words in the world, but if they weren't, Olivia couldn't think of anything that would make her heart swell or feel warmer, and make her want to move closer and be with someone. He loved her laugh? It was definitely a great start.

Chapter Twenty-Two

"I put extra marshmallows in it for you," Mark said, handing Olivia a mug of hot chocolate before he sat down across from her in an armchair, where she sat on the couch.

"How do you know I love marshmallows?"

"I overheard you saying it to someone a day or two ago. I think you were talking about how it's too bad that we didn't have enough hot chocolate to serve everyone in the activity center."

"Oh yeah. I remember. You were listening?"

"I seem to have Spidey senses when you're around. If you're talking, I want to hear what you're saying. If you're doing something, I want to watch. If you're laughing, I just want to absorb it."

Maybe he was being too mushy, or maybe he was being too honest. But he wasn't saying anything that wasn't true.

"Wow. I had no idea."

"I don't want to overwhelm you. And if you don't want to talk to me, it's fine. But I know I need to do something before my emotions get too invested and I can't think logically."

"No, that makes total sense to me. I know that's not exactly romantic, but maybe the romance can come later."

"Definitely the romance should come later. I've always thought that as humans we have it backwards, which is so true about so many things. We should do the logical things first, making sure that the person that we're considering spending the rest of our lives with doesn't believe in divorce, keeps her word, is committed to a godly marriage the way God intended, and so many more things. Instead, we run around looking for someone who looks good and who makes us feel good, and then we get married and we wonder why things fall apart." He paused, then he said, "But those marriages can still work. Sometimes, especially if both people are committed to them. But sometimes, one person just can't hold everything together, you know?"

She nodded. "I agree with you. It makes so much more sense the other way."

"And then, once people are married, there should be romance in their lives. It's not the sparkly, emotional, feel-good, hormonal, teenage type romance, but the kind of romance where you're constantly wanting to spend time with each other and date and talk and do fun things together. Little surprises, gifts, figuring out your love languages—all of those good things."

"I have to say that makes a lot of sense. I don't know that I've thought about it as deeply as you obviously have."

"As a pastor, I have to counsel couples, so I've thought about it. But also, I knew that I couldn't be dating ladies and breaking up with them, and just trying out people until I find someone who seems to fit me. And I fit her. Which seems to be how the American courting rituals are going now."

"True. I suppose you really did have to think about it for your job." She touched the rim of her mug, but didn't take a sip. "I have to be careful because of my boys. My job as a mom is to protect them. I have to watch who I bring into their lives, and, like you, I don't want to have a revolving door of men. Plus, I don't want to get involved with someone only to find out he's a jerk, and have him hurt my kids."

Mark nodded, thinking how amazing it was that she wasn't focused on herself, or either getting what she wanted, what she thought she deserved, or getting hurt by someone who wasn't a good person. Thoughts of herself hadn't even seemed to enter her mind. Her focus was all about doing the right thing for her boys.

"But I want to do what God wants me to do too. And I don't want to be afraid to move forward, if I'm sure that it's what God wants."

"Exactly. I've been praying about it a good bit. That's part of the reason why I wasn't afraid to say something. Because it seems to me that God has moved, arranging things so that you and I have been together. I don't believe in coincidences."

"I don't either."

He nodded, glad they were on the same page for that.

"Thank you for being willing to talk. I guess... I suppose that's a point in your favor, if we're keeping score, which I wasn't. I just really appreciate a man who is willing to sit down and discuss it, and doesn't just want to kiss and see if we're compatible physically."

He blinked. He wasn't expecting that kind of straight talk from her. "I guess that's true. Men do have a tendency to focus on that. But that's not the most important thing in a marriage, although... it's not unimportant."

To his relief, she nodded. "I agree. I think maybe especially to men. Not that it's not important to women either, it's just I think women have a tendency to be concerned about other things, like can he provide for me, will he protect me, is he going to turn out to be a jerk after he's decided that he's caught me and there's no chase for him anymore."

"Well, hopefully I don't turn out to be a jerk, but I think enough people know me that you can get some references if you want."

She gave a small smile. "I'm sorry. You're right. Your reputation in town is not that of a jerk. I guess... I just know so many people who thought they were marrying a good person, because he put on a good show, but after they were married, it's like he didn't really need to put the effort in anymore, and he turned into something she didn't sign up for."

"The reverse can be true as well."

She nodded.

"I hope that every day, every week, every month or whatever, as I live, I become a better person, not worse. And I do think that it's important, more than anything, to put your family first. I know more than one pastor who has lost his wife and children because he put his whole heart and soul into the ministry. And that's a good thing. After all, a pastor is doing God's work. But a pastor is still supposed to put his family first. Before the church, before the flock, before everything except his relationship with God. Family comes first."

It seemed like his words reassured her. He wasn't just saying them either. He believed that.

"I think I might appreciate family a little more than most people because I don't have any. My parents passed away, and I don't have any siblings. So many times I wish that there were lights on when I came home. You don't know how nice it's been the last couple of days to have you in the kitchen, humming a little, chatting with the boys, having them laugh and play and just feeling like I'm not alone in the world. You know?"

"Yeah. I guess sometimes I'm the opposite. I'd just like to have a little peace and quiet once in a while."

"That would be a benefit of having a husband, hopefully. Even if it's not me, your husband would take on some responsibility for the kids, and give you a little bit of time to yourself. It shouldn't be on your shoulders all the time."

"No. But I was thinking about what you had said about God giving us the ability to handle whatever He's put in front of us. As long as we're depending on Him. He's not going to give me a trial that He isn't expecting me to grow and become closer to Him through. And that's really where my focus needs to be. Not on the hardships of life, but on the person that I'm becoming because of it, and the relationship I have with Jesus."

"The pastor that I used to sit under used to say that when battles come, instead of looking at the enemy, you turn your eyes to Jesus. Expecting Him to fight for you, while you keep your eyes on Him."

"So just stand still and do nothing?"

"Well, there were a lot of times in the Bible God commanded his people to stand still and see the salvation of the Lord this day. And I do think that sometimes all we need to do is just keep being like Jesus, and God takes care of things. But no, I don't believe that we're not supposed to do anything. Most of the time, God wants us to do something. After all, how are we supposed to learn anything if we just stand around, and God does it all for us? It's kind of like a parent who never lets their child do anything, but does everything for them. Their kid never learns. Doesn't grow up, and they might be legally an adult, but they're technically still a baby, because they can't wash their own clothes, cook their own meals, or take care of themselves at all. It's sad, really."

"I agree that parents shouldn't do everything. And I do agree that a lot of times it's the mom who is the one wanting to baby their children far beyond when they should be."

"Well, I won't disagree with you, but a lot of times men allow their wives to dictate what's going to happen, and it's to the detriment of the children."

"I think that's because a lot of times relationships are unbalanced, and not biblical anymore. The woman is in charge, and the man has given up his natural authority, because he's scared that his wife is going to get mad at him, or do whatever, and so he just lets her do whatever she wants, and she ends up in control of the house."

"So you agree that the biblical directions for a home are correct?"

"I agree that God has a plan, including a plan for the home, and while we think we're modern, we think we know better than God, I disagree. I've never been successful when I ditched what God says and tried to do it my own way. I don't know why I would think for one second that His way wouldn't be best in this area, when it's best in every other area. After all, if I decide not to listen to God in this area, what else about the Bible am I gonna decide I don't agree with? And then, I'm putting myself ahead of God and saying that I know better, when nothing could be further from the truth. And the older I get, the more truth I see in that."

He sat still, a little stunned. She articulated that far better than he even could have. And he knew that if she didn't agree with the biblical mandate for marriage, where the husband was the head and the woman was submissive to the husband, while the husband loved the wife and gave himself for her the way Christ loved the church and gave himself for it, he wouldn't try to talk her into it. It would've been a no-go for him. But there she was, surprising him again.

That was the last piece, and everything settled down into his soul, and being with Olivia felt exactly right.

He wasn't so naïve as to think that Olivia had shed all of her doubts.

He cleared his throat. Where should he start?

"I am surprised to hear you say that, but I agree with you. But I do think that a lot of times in modern society men neglect their role. They think they're supposed to be the big boss in charge, and that the little lady is supposed to just do whatever he wants her to, and she ends up being a slave where he has her waiting on him hand and foot, because he's the king of the castle or whatever, and I don't agree with that at all. The Bible says that a man is supposed to love his wife the way Christ loved the church and gave himself for it. It also says that a man is supposed to dwell with his wife according to knowledge. That means a man is supposed to learn what his wife likes and dislikes, and to live with her according to that knowledge, catering to her likes and dislikes. And it also says that a man is supposed to love his wife the way he loves his own body, and cares for it. And the same way—just like I would not make myself... if I don't feel like jumping up and getting a drink of water or taking care of the children, then for me to command my wife to do that is wrong, because I'm not taking care of her the way I'm taking care of my own body, since my body is sitting on the couch being all comfortable. So, to expect her to wait on me, when I'm not waiting on her, is wrong. So, while I do believe that the woman is supposed to submit to the man and reverence him, and the man is the head of the home, that doesn't mean that the man is some king, and the woman is just his slave to be treated as such. She's supposed to have a place of honor at his side. But he does have the final say in the decisions, and if she doesn't agree with them, she goes along anyway."

Through all of that, Olivia had been nodding. Like she agreed with everything.

He had completely forgotten about his hot chocolate, because he'd been so engrossed in their conversation. And maybe even invested in it, because for the first time, he felt like she was the one. The one God had for him, the one God wanted him with, and the one who had been created for him.

But he had a lot at stake, because she had given no indications that she felt anything like that.

"Is there anything that we disagree on?" she asked, tilting her head and smiling a little. That smile gave him hope.

"I don't know about that, but as we were talking," he took a deep breath, because he was going to be laying himself out there, and if this didn't work out, these words were going to be out of his mouth and he could never take them back. "Everything seemed like it fell into place, and I felt like God was saying you were the one. Even before you agreed with that last thing I said, I felt like God was telling me to just trust Him and go with it." He blew a breath out. "But I don't expect you to make a decision that fast. Maybe God hasn't shown you anything, and maybe I'm just being hopeful, because I really, really like you."

He wasn't sure what else to say, so he shut up. He wasn't the slightest bit hungry, and although he loved hot chocolate, he let his sit on the coffee table. Waiting.

Chapter Twenty-Three

Olivia sat on the couch across from Mark, trying to squelch the growing hope in her chest. Could this really be the man God had for her? Could he really be interested in marrying her? Her? Someone who had absolutely zero qualifications to be a pastor's wife... They needed to talk about that.

"You're a pastor. You need a wife who is going to help you in the ministry. I have no qualifications and absolutely no skill in that area."

He leaned back a little, seeming to be confident now, his arm casually leaning on the armrest of the chair, his eyes always on her.

It was funny—that didn't make her nervous. It actually made her feel warm and... seen in a way that she hadn't felt seen in a long time.

"I think you're perfect."

That was it? That was all he was going to say? She hadn't quite figured out how to answer him when he continued.

"You're right, I would hope that my wife would be willing to help me in the ministry. Being a pastor is really a family occupation. Our kids would be involved in church, my wife would be involved in church. It's not the kind of job where I go to work and no one else ever sees anything that I do. It's the kind of job where I need my family with me. People are going to be looking at me and my family, and judging us based on our actions. I suppose you might want to think twice, whether or not you want to be involved in that. Sometimes it's like living in a fishbowl. People expect to be able to walk into your house," he waved around the living room, where she knew that people had been in and out all week as they stayed in the activity center. "People knock on my door, all hours of the night. Sometimes they need a bed, sometimes they just need food, sometimes they're having a domestic emergency. They'll call me over —a couple who's having marital issues will call me to their house as they're throwing plates at each other and threatening to hurt each other."

She shuddered. Unable to imagine such a thing. She had gotten mad at Cam more than once in their marriage, but throwing plates?

"You're kidding, right?" she finally said.

One corner of his mouth turned up. He shook his head. "No, unfortunately, I am not."

"Were you able to help?" she asked, thinking that maybe she wasn't as worldly as what she thought. After all, she'd never seen a domestic dispute where people were actually throwing things at each other. Yelling and screaming, and getting in their car and storming off, yes, but throwing stuff?

"No. Unfortunately, that couple divorced, and the wife had to get a restraining order against the husband... actually, the husband had to get a restraining order against the wife."

"The husband?" she asked, shocked again.

He nodded. "Do you see why I need to protect myself? That's why we had to have this talk."

She laughed. Able to tell by his tone that he was joking.

"I think it sounds like there are some really scary women in the world."

"There are. Sometimes I feel like the women are worse than the men, although I know that's mostly not true. Although... I do think toxic feminism has decimated a lot of homes. I know I could get in a lot of trouble for saying that, but it's true."

She nodded. She could understand what he was saying. Women had a tendency to take over and start bossing.

"I don't think that really applies to us, though," he said. And he wasn't asking a question, he was making a statement, like he was confident about her.

"Thanks." Her word was soft. He looked up, a bit of surprise in his eyes at her tone.

"You thought I would think that about you?"

She lifted a shoulder. "I guess you don't know me very well."

"I think I know you better than you think I do. I might have been talking to a few people about you. Not in a gossiping kind of way, but in a 'I like her a lot, and I'm trying to find out a little bit more about her before I approach her' kind of way."

"Okay."

"I guess we were talking about my job, and how if you were going to be with me... we're talking about marriage, right?"

She took a breath and nodded. That's what they were talking about. The M word. It was funny—when she was younger and getting married to Cam, she didn't really give it much thought. But after she was married, she realized exactly how trapped she was. If someone made a bad mistake and married the wrong person, the Bible didn't really give them much of an out. They pretty much had to make the best of it. Modern teaching tickled people's ears and made it seem otherwise, but there was no Biblical out for someone in a marriage, other than adultery. Jesus was very, very clear about that. And even in the case of adultery, Olivia wasn't entirely sure that God wouldn't want them to try to stay and make the best of it.

Marriage was indeed for life.

"Yes. We're talking about marriage. It's a lifetime commitment. Not one I take lightly."

"Me neither. And that's important."

She nodded. She didn't want someone who wasn't completely committed.

"I can't be a pastor and be divorced. Well, I suppose I can be divorced, but I can't remarry. Regardless, I don't want to have divorce be a part of my vocabulary. If we get married, I want us to do whatever we need to in order to make things work. Whatever we need."

"All right. I agree with that. I don't want to be divorced, and I don't believe in it, unless we're looking at adultery, and even then I'm not entirely sure that God wouldn't rather we forgive and try to work and keep the marriage and family together. He talks a lot about that in the Old Testament, when he compares Israel to an adulterous woman. He always wants her to come back to him."

"Very good. I'm impressed with your biblical knowledge. I don't know why you think that you wouldn't be a perfect pastor's wife."

"I don't feel the slightest bit qualified."

"I'm pretty sure that is what makes you exceptionally qualified. If you were confident that you could do it, if you thought you deserved that teaching position and thought that you had a lot to offer other people, I guess I would question it. Not that I would say that you didn't—it's just... there's a lot of pride involved in that."

"Yeah. I can see what you're saying, but I'm serious. I don't know the Bible that well, not like I think a pastor's wife should."

"Well, there is something that you're going to have to deal with. A lot of times people hold a pastor's wife to a higher standard than they hold anyone else."

She closed her mouth and leaned back, a little surprised. He was right. People did hold pastor's wives to a higher standard, and if she got married to Mark, she would be the pastor's wife!

People would hold her to a higher standard!

"Wow. That's just sunk in."

"Well, it's a good thing to think about. Because once we're married, you can't get out of it. And I can't change it. People are going to expect you to be super spiritual, they're gonna want you to be held to a higher standard than anyone else. They're gonna want your kids to be more spiritual than anyone else's kids. And anything that your kids do, that you do, that you wear, that you say, that you go—it's all going to be held under the microscope."

"Wow. Okay. You're right. I do that myself, and now I see how wrong it was, but there's no changing it, and there's no way I'm gonna be able to get people to not do it to me. I guess in a way I deserve it."

He shook his head.

"No, I definitely wouldn't say you deserve it, but it's true."

"I've never noticed that you seem to resent or are affected in any way by the fact that people probably do hold you to a higher moral and religious standard than anyone else."

"I guess I just feel like I want to be held to that high standard. I want people to be watching me. I want to know that there are people following me, that will help me stay strong and stay true. I mean, I want to do right just because I love Jesus, but sometimes the flesh tempts you to do things that you shouldn't, and it's so helpful to me to know that there are people around me watching me, holding me to that high standard, and that if I fall, it's going to be really bad for me."

"So you're not perfect?" she asked, tilting her head and narrowing her eyes a bit. It wasn't that she thought he was perfect, she just couldn't imagine him being tempted to do wrong.

"Not even close."

"You just seem so... I guess maybe not perfect but just really close."

"Well, don't get confused, because I'm not. I'm not perfect, and I know I'm never going to be, but hopefully every day, I'm a little more like Jesus than I was the day before. Isn't that the goal?"

"It is."

They sat there for a little bit, and she didn't know what he was thinking, but she was trying to figure out if there was anything else they needed to go over. She knew that marrying him would mean he would want her in the church, leading Sunday school and ladies' groups and making meals and donating her time and efforts towards his ministry. And... she was okay with that. She just needed to think about her children, and honestly, she thought it would be really good for them. She had been a little bit concerned about them growing up on a military base and in a military family, because there were a lot of bad influences. This would be almost a one eighty.

"So where does that leave us?" he asked, and his question filled the warmth and coziness of the house. Demanding an answer, vibrating almost in an audible way.

Before she could say anything, his phone rang.

"I'm sorry, I forgot to turn it off. If you and I are having an important conversation, I don't want anything else to interfere with it."

"Go ahead and answer it. Maybe we just need to think about things for a little bit."

He looked at her like that really wasn't what he wanted her to say, and honestly, she'd rather get things settled. But if she was going to be a pastor's wife, he wasn't going to be able to drop everything for her all the time. And there were going to be times where he was going to get calls and he was going to have to leave her, or come back to her later. That was just the nature of his job. She appreciated the fact that he was going to try to make time for her, though. Still.

"Go on. Answer it."

Chapter Twenty-Four

Mark really didn't want to stop talking before they had hashed things out, but Olivia was probably right. They probably should take some time to think about it, but more than that, to pray about it. After all, as far as he was concerned, it wasn't his decision to make. He'd already decided that God wanted him with Olivia, so there wasn't anything for him to think about other than was he going to do what God wanted, or was he going to give in to his worldly fears and take things slow and be cautious? Was he afraid of getting hurt? Was he afraid that Olivia wouldn't be perfect? Because she wasn't going to be perfect.

He slid his phone on and said, "Hello?" He had forgotten to look to see who it was.

"Mark." It was Noah. "I know that you've been busy doing some Secret Saint activities all day, which goes along really well with your job, but I just found out about a family who's been stranded in the snow since before it began. No electricity, no heat, and they're running out of food."

"Okay. I've got some groceries left from what everyone brought for the church. I can run those out yet tonight. And—"

"That would be perfect. I don't suppose there's any leftover soup?"

"I've got some homemade bread here. And... yeah. It's not leftover, Olivia just made it tonight."

"Olivia is there?" Noah asked, sounding surprised.

"Yeah. You should have been able to see that her side of the street didn't have electricity until just a bit ago."

"Oh. Yeah. I guess I wasn't thinking about where she was staying. She seems so self-contained."

"She does. But that doesn't mean she is." He glanced at Olivia, who sat in the chair, staring at her feet. Maybe she didn't want to look like she was eavesdropping. He felt bad that he was making her uncomfortable.

And then he realized that she might be curious about what he was talking about. What was he going to say?

"All right. I'll text you the address. Are you sure you'll be able to get out tonight?"

"How hard is it going to be to get into their driveway?"

"They've been working to shovel it, although they're not finished. They have a small path to walk on, not driveable. But if they know that you're coming, they'll be out there to meet you. They have one cell phone that has not died yet, and they're being very judicious about its use, but I can text them and let them know. Or I can give you the cell phone number, and you can let them know what time you'll be at the end of the driveway."

"All right. That sounds good. I have a few things I need to wrap up here, so it's going to be a little bit. But if you give me their number, I'll text them."

"All right. Thanks a lot."

They hung up, and Mark looked at his phone for a minute before he lifted his eyes to Olivia.

"I'm sorry. I wasn't sure whether I should stay or leave."

"I guess... I guess that's something else we need to talk about. I don't believe that a married couple should have secrets about anything. Other than maybe Christmas or special occasion gifts that are meant to be a surprise, but not hidden secrets that we're keeping from each other."

"I agree. But in your role as pastor, there will probably be things you're going to be talking to people about that you can't talk to me about."

"I've never run into this problem before, and I'm not sure what I'll do about it, but I guess I want to present the two of us as together... So, especially if I were to be counseling a female, I would want you in the room with me."

She blinked, as though that surprised her.

"Why?"

"I don't think it's a good idea for a man and a woman to be in a closed room together. Not only could I lose my ministry if it was her word against mine that something happened, but you don't want anything to happen, and you don't want to give yourself the opportunity. Being in a closed room with a female could put you at risk. I don't want to risk my marriage for anything. It's more important to me than anything else in the world, other than my relationship with Jesus, and that would affect my relationship with Jesus."

She nodded. She understood what he was saying. It was better to not give oneself the opportunity to sin at all. And maybe that seemed a little odd.

"I agree that there should be no secrets. I do think that if someone tells you something in confidence, that's a little bit different, but I also think that you're right about being in a closed room. I had never considered that before, but it's not something that comes up in my line of work."

He kind of wanted to talk to her about her line of work. She had said on previous occasions that she only worked because she had to. He wondered how she felt about continuing to work. He didn't want to tell her she had to, or tell her that she couldn't. But he wanted her to do what worked best for her, and for the ministry.

"So can I know what that phone call was about?" she asked.

He lifted his brows, and then a little smile turned up the corners of his mouth. "What I'm about to tell you, no one else in town knows other than Noah."

"Okay," she said, sounding curious but also cautious.

"Have you heard of the Secret Saint activities?"

"Yeah. Everyone in town has."

"That's me. And I have a partner."

"You're the Secret Saint?" she asked, her eyes getting big and her brows going up.

"Yeah. Hopefully that's okay?"

"Wow. I'm... I'm shocked. I guess it makes a lot of sense, though. Although, how long have you been the Secret Saint, because you just became the pastor this fall."

"My other church wasn't that far away. Only about forty-five minutes. And since I had no family, and since I'm a pastor, and I have a tendency to get around and know things other people don't, I've been helping. Pastor Johnson had recommended me to some of the other people who have been the Secret Saint over the years."

"So it hasn't been you all along?"

"No. I think some people have gotten married, and when you start to have a wife and children, it becomes a little bit harder to sneak around in the middle of the night."

"Yeah, that kind of looks suspicious in some ways."

"Yeah. But honestly, I don't even know who all the Secret Saints were. I just know who my partner is now."

"I don't need to know that."

"I was just talking to him. Like I said, I don't think there should be secrets between us if we're going to be married. Is that what we're looking at still?" He supposed that they weren't married yet—maybe he didn't need to out Noah—but he was feeling pretty confident. Maybe she wouldn't do what God wanted her to, or maybe he was dead wrong about what God wanted, but he was more certain than he'd ever been about anything other than his call to preach, that he was supposed to marry Olivia.

"Yes. That's what we're talking about. And I know I said we could think about it, but I'm convinced. I know this is what God wants. And for me to fiddle and fuddle around would just be me not having faith that God's gonna work everything out. I can't say that I have no fear—that I'm not scared—but I can say that I have total confidence in God's plan, and I know my part is to just walk forward, without concern for anything but doing what God wants."

He nodded, feeling satisfied.

"Can I ask where you're going?"

"The Hodge family, outside of town."

She drew her brows together, and then tilted her head. "Aren't those the people who left the church when they found out that the church had decided that you would be the next pastor? And they took three other families with them?"

He nodded slowly, his stomach still curling at the thought, but he knew what God wanted him to do. He'd forgiven them long ago, and now was his chance to not just prove it, but to do something kind for them. What did the Bible say about heaping coals of fire upon their heads? "That's the family."

"And you're taking your own food out of your own refrigerator to them?"

"Well, part of it is stuff that you made. So if you don't want me to, I won't."

"No. It has nothing to do with me. They just were very, very mean to you."

"And that's true. But the Bible says that we're to be kind to people who are unkind to us. That we're to turn the other cheek. That we are to allow vengeance to be the Lord's. I mean, the Bible is full of forgiving people for what they've done, allowing God to handle it, and loving them and being kind to them anyway. I wouldn't be a very good pastor if I didn't practice that, would I?"

She shook her head slowly.

"But I don't want you to think that it's easy. I spent a lot of nights lying awake, wondering if I'd even have a church because of all the rumors that were flying around and the lies that those people told about me. I can't say that it doesn't still hurt, that I don't still get a twinge whenever I think about them. But I don't have to feel perfectly happy in order to do the right thing, right?"

She nodded her head, and he knew she wouldn't argue with him. She knew he was right. There was no way she could present the other side using the Bible, because it just wasn't there.

"I'd love to have you go along, but I know you can't leave the boys." He lifted a shoulder. "I know Mrs. Tucker has said to me that she'll come give me a hand anytime."

"And she's offered to watch the boys multiple, multiple times, and has. I just hate to bother her."

"I don't think it's a bother. She's retired, and she feels like she's not as useful as she used to be. She looks for things to do to be a blessing. You're actually giving her a blessing by allowing her to help you."

"I'll keep that in mind. Thank you." She sighed. "I'll wait up for you."

"You don't have to." But he couldn't stop the surge of pleasure that went through him at the idea that there would be somebody waiting at home, keeping the lights on, waiting to welcome him, caring whether he made it or not. It had been so long since there was anything like that.

"No. I want to make sure you get back okay, for one. And... I just want to see you again."

He smiled, and swallowed, then he put his hand on her knee. Immediately she put her hand over top of his, and their fingers twined together.

He wanted to say something, tell her that he was falling in love with her, that he did love her, that he would always love her, but he felt like it was too soon. The world didn't think that a person could love someone so deeply and so fiercely after such a short time. But biblical love didn't have anything to do with one's feelings. It had to do with decisions a person made, and a commitment a person had, and a person's character as well. He could've said that he loved her before he even met her, and then his actions could've confirmed that that was true. Still, he didn't think that they were ready for another deep discussion about love.

So he just squeezed her hand and then stood. "I'll be back as quickly as I can."

"Be careful."

Chapter Twenty-Five

Olivia sat on the couch long after Mark had left. Taking food to those people who had been so mean to him. Meaner to him than anyone had ever been to her. Including her parents.

And yet years later, she was still angry at her parents and not including them in her life or in her children's lives because of them warning her, fairly, that Cam might not be the best decision she ever made. Why had she been so stubborn and stupid? Not necessarily for not listening to them—she had considered herself in love, and hadn't thought for one second that Cam was anything like her parents were afraid he was. But she hadn't needed to cut her parents out of her life. Especially after Cam passed.

She touched her phone, running her finger over the edge of it, thinking.

Her stomach twisted, and she almost drew her hand back, but instead, she gripped her phone where it lay on the coffee table, and picked it up.

The number was still in her contacts, although she honestly didn't even know if they were still alive. She'd blocked it long ago and had tried not to think about them since. Her boys didn't even know they had grandparents.

How could she have been so terrible?

Somehow talking to Mark had made her see what an awful person she had been. Not just a terrible daughter, but a terrible Christian, a terrible child of God. How could she claim that God was her father and Jesus was her savior when she couldn't even forgive her own parents? And show love to them, when Jesus said that they'll know that we're Christians by our love.

Mark lived that out. He was showing love to people who had been terribly unkind to him, and he hadn't even given it a thought. He agreed immediately to take food to them. He was risking his life —he could get stuck, he could get lost in the snow since the whole countryside looked pretty much the same.

She wasn't going to borrow trouble. Saying a prayer that he would be safe, and being convicted even more strongly that before she asked God for one more thing, she needed to get rid of this thing that was between her parents and her, she unlocked her phone and went to her keypad.

It wasn't hard to remember her old number. The one she'd had for her whole childhood, but her finger hovered over the buttons. It would ring in her parents' house, and either one of them could answer it. Unless they changed their number or moved or whatever people did.

She glanced at the clock. She didn't think they would be asleep yet. Her parents had always been late-night owls.

Before she could think herself out of it, she dialed their number.

She held her breath while it rang once, twice, three times.

Telling herself she'd let it ring one more time before she hung up, and rapidly losing her nerve, she almost dropped her phone when she heard her mom's voice say, "Hello?"

Did they even recognize her number?

"Mom, it's Olivia." There was silence on the line. It felt like forever.

"Harold! It's Olivia!" Her mom said, excitement making her voice tremble. "Harold! Harold! Pick up the other phone!"

"Olivia! Oh, my baby, how are you?"

"I'm just fine. I'm sorry. I was unkind and my meanness was uncalled for, and I'm sorry." There. She got it out. If they were gonna be mad at her, at least she'd apologized.

"You don't have anything to be sorry for. You're our daughter. We love you." It was her dad. Good—he heard it so she didn't have to do it twice.

Wait. Just like that?

"You guys aren't going to be mad at me?" she asked, unbelieving. She hadn't talked to them for five years. Surely they were going to make her pay something, and it wasn't just as easy as saying "we forgive you, come back into our lives."

"He's right. You're our daughter. We're just thrilled that you're actually talking to us. Although I'm a little scared. I don't want to do anything that's going to make you mad again." Her mom sounded worried.

"No, Mom. I'm over that. I was immature and stupid. And nothing you do is going to make me mad. I promise." She hoped she could keep that promise. But really, her parents obviously loved her. They wanted a relationship with her, and it had been her all along, keeping them away.

"I need to know everything. Where have you been? What have you been doing? We haven't heard a thing."

"Why don't you come visit me for Christmas, and we can talk about it all then."

"Where are you? We'll be there." That was her dad.

"We settled down in Mistletoe Meadows, Virginia."

"You've been so close all this time!" her mom said.

"Give us the address. When would you like us to show up?"

She didn't want to get into the situation with her furnace, but she couldn't have her parents coming when it didn't work.

"How about Monday? You can stay as long as you want to, even if it's over Christmas."

"Yes. Thank you. What can we bring?"

"Just bring yourselves. My boys would like to see you." They would be thrilled to find out they had grandparents.

"You have boys?"

"Twin boys. They're four. Cam died before they were born. He didn't even know I was pregnant."

"Oh, Olivia. Why didn't you tell us?" her mom said.

"I have a lot of things to tell you guys. But I do think it'll go better if you just show up. We can talk as much as you want."

"We'll be there. Monday. Do the boys like anything in particular?"

"No. They're just boys. You don't have to bring them anything. They're just gonna be thrilled to know that they have grandparents."

"Who love them. I can't wait to meet them! What are their names?"

She should've known that her mom would want all the details.

She chatted about them for just a little bit, and then, promising to tell her parents everything, and saying that she wanted to know all the things that were going on with them, they hung up.

It was amazing how much lighter she felt. How much better.

Would she still feel that way if it hadn't gone as well?

She had a feeling she would. If she would've called, apologized, admitted what she had done wrong, and asked for forgiveness, even if her parents had been mad and refused to talk to her, she would've felt so much better. Just getting it off her chest. She hadn't realized how that was bogging her down.

Feeling content and happy, she turned all the lights out, except for a dim one above the stove in the kitchen and the Christmas tree in the corner of the living room, and then sat down on Mark's couch, smelling his familiar scent, and thanking God for his influence in her life. If it hadn't been for him, she probably wouldn't have called her parents this Christmas. And it would've been one more Christmas that she would've lost to anger and bitterness.

Her parents already had missed the first four years of her children's lives, and it was all her fault. But she could try as hard as she could to be more like Jesus—forgiving, no matter what. Because wasn't that what He did? People who were terribly unkind to him, who were putting him to death, were the very people He was dying to save. If that had been her, it would've been a no-go. She would've told them they could go find a different savior, and she would've turned her back and walked away from them. From her. But Jesus didn't. And it wasn't really that she was supposed to be a better version of herself. She was supposed to be more like Jesus. That was the goal.

Chapter Twenty-Six

Several hours later, Olivia still had her Bible open on her lap and had been reading it and talking to God. She hadn't completely alleviated all of her doubts and fears, but the idea that she would be with Mark was absolutely clear in her mind.

She smiled as she stood up and walked to the window as she heard his vehicle pulling into the church parking lot.

There probably would be many nights like this, where he needed to go help someone in the church, and she was home by herself. Was she okay with that?

But the answer was clear. It didn't matter whether she was okay with it or not. If this was the calling that God placed on her life, if it was true that she was supposed to marry him, and she thought it was, then it didn't matter. She would have to make it work, she would have to be okay with it. God would help her do whatever needed to be done.

It seemed like an insurmountable task. The amount of help that people needed, and she was just one person. But together with Mark, they would be more than the two of them individually, and although

God didn't necessarily need them, He wanted them to work for Him. She looked forward to it.

She hurried to the door and stood there as Mark walked in, his cheeks rosy, his hat pulled down close over his forehead, his shoulders hunched from the cold.

"Man, it's cold out there!" he said as he walked in, seeing her. His eyes twinkled, and his face broke into a smile.

"Welcome back. I have some water heating. Hot chocolate?"

"Yes please."

But she didn't make any move to go get it. She didn't have many doubts—but she still had a curl of nervousness, a little fear. This was a huge step, and she and Mark did not know each other very well. But God knew them both, and if God ordained this, then she was a fool to not walk forward in His timing.

"I'll take your coat," she said as he unzipped it.

He nodded, grabbing his hat from his head and shrugging out of his coat.

But instead of handing it to her, he threw it over the back of the chair and stepped forward.

She paused for just a moment, and then stepped into his embrace, his arms coming around her, and it felt like coming home. Right and perfect and like it was meant to be.

He looked at her face, and he smiled down at her.

"I missed you."

"I missed you too. But I did something while you were gone."

"Yes?" he asked, their faces just inches apart.

"I called my parents. I apologized to them for being such a brat, and they're coming on Monday."

"Then we're gonna get your furnace fixed by then. I wouldn't want them to think that we're living together."

"No one's gonna think that. The whole town knows my furnace isn't working, I'm sure by now. We will get it figured out."

"Yeah. We."

"Yeah. It's us now."

He nodded.

"How did your trip go?"

"I actually think they're coming to church on Sunday." He said it while still shaking his head a little, like he was still a little amazed. "It never fails to shock me how God works in people's hearts. But... they apologized to me. I don't get that very much as a pastor. I think people think they can just kind of take advantage of me and it doesn't really matter. And I was acting like there was nothing wrong."

"I think if they're truly Christians, they feel guilty for what they've done. I know I did. Although it took me a little while."

"Sometimes we just don't think about things, because we don't like the way we feel when we do."

"Yeah. I was definitely avoiding it."

"So we each had a pretty good evening."

"Yeah. I spent a little time praying and reading my Bible, and I feel good about this." She indicated their embrace and the two of them.

"I'm thrilled to hear it. I kind of figured I got to that point a little bit before you did." He paused, and then he sounded a lot less confident when he said, "Is it okay if I kiss you?"

"I was hoping you would." It wasn't exactly the reason why she'd waited up, but it might've been part of it.

He smiled before his head lowered, and his lips met hers. She melted into him, feeling warm and safe and a spark of something that could only be the attraction that she felt for Mark fanning into a flame. Kissing Mark was definitely better than thinking about it.

It didn't last long. He lifted his head shortly after and rested his forehead on hers.

"Will you marry me?" he said, their noses almost touching. Almost immediately he apologized. "That was terrible. I'm sorry. You deserve a better proposal than that."

"No. I don't want a better proposal, I want that proposal. It was perfect. And yes. I would love to marry you. The sooner the better."

She grinned up into his eyes, realizing that all the nervousness and fear that she had, the uncertainty, the idea that this was a huge decision and she should take a lot of time to think about it—all melted away. She didn't need a lot of time. In fact, she'd read somewhere that taking a lot of time to make a decision actually made a person make a worse decision. All she needed to know was that Mark was going to do everything in his power to be the best husband he could, and that she was going to do everything in her power to be the best wife she could. And that God wanted them together. Beyond that, it would all work out. It had to. It might not be easy, it might be downright hard at times, but she wasn't afraid of a little work, and she wasn't afraid of a little uncomfortableness either. Not if she was doing what God wanted her to.

"How about that hot chocolate?" she asked.

"All right. I guess I was just standing here, holding you, feeling happy down to my toes and back. I'll do my best to be the best husband I possibly can to you. I guess being the best husband probably means trying to be as much like Jesus as possible."

"I think so. I think that's where we get confused sometimes. We try to be the best version of ourselves, and it's not about that. It's about becoming more like Jesus. That's how we become better people."

"I couldn't agree more. And I'm blessed to have such a wise and thoughtful fiancée."

The Christmas tree sparkled in the corner, and the scent of hot chocolate drifted into the air, but neither one of them noticed as his head lowered and his lips touched hers again.

Chapter Twenty-Seven

Mark felt like he was walking on air for the next couple of days, as he spent as much time as humanly possible with Olivia, while still doing everything he could to help the church and do his Secret Saint activities. There were practices for the music ensemble, amateur carpenters coming and going as they built the platform, questions to answer as the marketing committee worked on a plan to continue to sell more tickets. Although word-of-mouth had gotten out, and the sale of tickets had already exceeded their hopes, and more than paid for everything, including the candles.

Olivia didn't seem to be too anxious about the fact that she wasn't getting the candles made that needed to be made.

The furnace repairman had not been able to come the first day, but he said he would come the day after.

Mark admitted to Olivia that he was not disappointed. And that he loved having them in his house and home and really didn't want them to leave.

He knew they needed to. He certainly couldn't seem like he was living with his fiancée, no matter how separate their bedrooms were.

Plus, he had to admit it was a temptation to have her there anyway.

"What about a Christmas wedding?" he asked that evening after the children were in bed.

He'd had such a great time playing with them in the living room, and Olivia had joined in, then sat on a chair and read a book while he continued. Apparently, men enjoyed playing for a much longer time than women did.

Or maybe she just enjoyed seeing him with her children. That was what she claimed anyway.

"Like, next-week Christmas wedding?" Olivia asked, her brows raised in surprise.

"Is that too soon?" he asked.

"No. I'll marry you today if you want me to."

"You don't want to plan something big and flashy?"

"No. I had a big first wedding, and maybe flashy isn't the right word, but it didn't help our marriage be any better, no matter how much money we spent on it. And I'm just not interested in that anymore. I have other things I'd rather spend our money on, for one, and I just don't feel like a big wedding equals a great marriage. Plus, I have candles to make. I don't have time to plan a wedding." She bit her lip. "Unless you want one?" Her brow was all crinkled up, and she seemed truly concerned about what he wanted.

Somehow, that made him happy. That she really cared about what he thought and wanted.

"I just want to marry you. I don't really care how it happens. And I want it to be soon."

"Then we agree on all of that."

He smiled, squeezing her hand as they sat on the couch together.

But before he could try to pin down a day with her, his phone rang.

"I don't need to get it," he said as he looked at her.

"Go ahead. It's your job."

He nodded. "Unfortunately that's probably the way it's going to go. Some evenings we'll have together, uninterrupted, and some evenings not."

"God knows. I guess if I start to feel neglected or like I'm alone too much, I'll let you know."

"Fair enough. As long as you promise not to suffer in silence without talking to me."

"I know that you'll do something about it if I say something, and that's important to me."

"Fair enough," he said as he reached in his pocket and pulled out his phone.

"Hello?"

"Hey, it's Noah," Noah said.

"What's up?" Mark asked, his stomach sinking a little as he realized that Noah probably had something he wanted him to deliver as a Secret Saint thing.

"I've got a problem and I was wondering if I could come talk to you about it."

"You can. Olivia is here... I can go to my office if you want, or if you don't mind if she listens in, you can come to the living room."

"She can hear, as long as she doesn't say anything. It's probably not something that I want getting around."

"All right. You can come then. Show up whenever."

"All right, I'll be right over."

He hung up and sat holding his phone for a minute, wondering what in the world Noah would want to talk to him about.

"That was Noah?"

"Yes."

"It didn't sound like he had a Secret Saint delivery for you."

"No. He wants to come talk."

"I can leave. I can head to bed." Olivia volunteered, and he appreciated so much that she didn't need to know every single thing that people were telling him. That would make his job as a pastor much easier. But he also intended to let people know that he considered Olivia and him one, and he didn't want to keep secrets from her. He wasn't sure how he was going to balance that with counseling, but he'd cross those bridges when he came to them.

"I'll put some hot chocolate on."

"Okay," he said, standing up with her. He'd rather spend the last few minutes cuddling on the couch with her, but he appreciated the fact that she wanted to make his guest feel welcome too. He hadn't had that at all in his ministry, and it felt good to be able to offer his guest something when they came in.

Noah arrived, accepted the hot chocolate, and they were settled on the couch not too long afterwards.

"This doesn't have anything to do with the Secret Saint thing, does it?" Mark started, just because Noah seemed to have a hard time trying to figure out what to say.

"No. It has to do with one of my siblings. You know I raised them."

"You did a great job," Mark said.

"Thanks. It's only by the grace of God. I certainly wasn't qualified to do anything."

"I don't know. I guess that's true."

"So it's about Ty."

"The second oldest, right?"

"That's correct."

"Is he in trouble?"

"I don't think so. I just got a really weird phone call from him today, and I told him I needed to think about it and pray about it before I gave him advice. Although my first instinct was to tell him to run in a different direction."

"All right, go ahead. Start wherever you need to," Mark said, wanting to encourage him to talk, not feel like he had to have a perfect story put together.

"Apparently he's met a woman who has proposed a marriage of convenience. I didn't even know there was such a thing, but he explained to me that they're not dating. They haven't even met in person. They've met online, and she wants to get married without all the trappings of modern dating or all of that. She just wanted someone who shared her values and morals, and he hasn't even seen what she looks like."

"Wow. I didn't realize that was a thing."

"I didn't either. But apparently there's a website. I don't know what my brother was doing on it."

"Well, that's a good question. Has he been longing to get married and just couldn't find anyone?"

"I didn't think so. But it's true that he's not married, and he's almost as old as I am."

"I see. I don't think that men kind of have the ticking clock the way women do," Mark said, glancing at Olivia, who shrugged her shoulders. She didn't seem to have a ticking clock. He didn't think that she was even looking for a husband and was kind of surprised by their relationship. But he didn't know for sure.

"I don't know what to tell him. I've asked him all the questions— is she a Christian, does she have references that you can talk to, people who know about how she acts and whether she acts like a Christian, and whether she has fruit, and what her character's like. He said he's checked her out."

"And he hasn't seen a picture?" Mark asked, shocked. "In today's world, everyone has their photos on social media."

"No. No picture. Apparently she doesn't do social media."

"But somehow he found out that she wanted a marriage of convenience?"

"It was a website." Noah lifted a shoulder like he really wasn't sure exactly what was going on.

"But he's checked around, talked to her references? Has he met any of the people that know her?"

"He visited her town. Apparently. He hasn't met with her yet, because he didn't want to even see her if she didn't check out. Then, after he had checked her out himself, he came to me and said that he wanted to get married. He wasn't going to agree to marry her without talking to me about it. Which I appreciate, but... I don't know what to say." Noah leaned his forearms on his knees and rubbed his hands together. "I've run into a lot of odd things raising my siblings, but this takes the cake as the thing that has stumped me the hardest. Even the girl stuff I managed to muddle my way through."

"I've gotta say, I guess I haven't been a pastor as long as Pastor Johnson has, but this is a first for me too."

"So what do I do?" Noah asked, looking at Mark like he had all the answers.

"I guess, even though it's a first for us, the Bible hasn't changed. God doesn't really give any specifications for marriage other than they have to be a believer. Beyond that, we seem to be able to pick for ourselves. Does he really want to just choose, for his lifetime mate and partner, someone he's going to be one with in the eyes of God, as someone he's never even seen? Someone he doesn't know at all? But with that said, he checked out the most important thing—that she's a believer. So biblically, I think it's okay. Humanly, I don't know that I would recommend it. But Ty has a brain. I've always thought that he was rather practical, and maybe this is just taking that kind of practicality into a whole new level. I'm just surprised he found a woman to go along with it. Or who actually suggested it."

"I guess that's the way I was leaning too. I want to say no, but I have no Bible to back me up. So I guess I have to say... do it at your own risk. Just remember, marriage is forever. So if it doesn't work out, you're going to spend the rest of your life trying as hard as you can to stay married. And maybe not being very happy, or choosing to be happy despite the fact that maybe it wasn't an ideal thing."

"Yeah. I guess I agree with you. I... know that that's not the way our society works, but just because it's not the way we do things in our society doesn't make it wrong. In fact, years ago, arranged marriages were a normal thing. People didn't pick their own mates —they had someone chosen for them, and then they learned to love each other and get along. That's just the way it was."

"That's what I thought too."

Through all of this, Olivia had been quiet, but she finally spoke up. "I know no one asked me, but—"

"You're always welcome to give your opinion," Mark quickly said. He wasn't used to having a woman beside him, and he needed to make sure that he showed her more deference in the future. He'd apologize later.

"That's fine. He came to talk to you. But I guess I would say she must be desperate. Either she doesn't have money, or she doesn't have security, or there's something else going on. But Ty always seemed like the kind of person who wanted to help, and so maybe that's what's driving him. He feels needed."

"I hadn't considered that, but it's a good idea. And it makes it make sense, which was something I was struggling with."

They talked for a bit more, but they didn't come to a different conclusion. It wasn't wrong, even if society was going to think it was crazy. Society wasn't their standard—the Bible was. And that was the way it was supposed to be.

Chapter Twenty-Eight

The next couple of days went by quickly, as they waited for her furnace to be repaired and stayed busy—busier than Olivia had ever been. She made soup for needy people in the community, while Mark continued to help people who were still shut in, visiting them, doing Secret Saint activities. And both of them were involved in the activities at the church, practicing for the various Christmas festivities and taking care of her children.

Usually, they found a few minutes in the evening to get back together and to chat, but several times Mark had to go out for Secret Saint activities while she stayed home, wrapping gifts that he was coming back to pick up and deliver.

She loved that life and thought that it would be a very good one, but she wouldn't have minded seeing Mark more. However, she reminded herself that there weren't typically storms as big as this one, and this was probably not going to be a typical schedule.

They decided not to tell anyone that they were engaged on Sunday, but they did figure that they could allow their relationship to become public. Mark was careful to let everyone know that she was only staying in the guest room until her furnace was repaired, although he said nothing from the pulpit. As he explained to her, the pulpit was for church business, not his personal business.

She couldn't agree more.

The reaction from the congregation was almost exclusively positive. She had caught a couple of side looks, but she honestly didn't know what they meant. Maybe people just couldn't imagine that the pastor would like someone like her. And it had nothing to do with her staying in his house until her furnace was repaired. Thankfully, the repairman came early Monday morning, and they spent Monday afternoon moving her and the boys back into their house.

"I've managed not to stress about getting the candles made this entire time. There was nothing I could do, you know? But now that I'm back in here, I feel a little overwhelmed at all the work I have to do."

"I told you I would help you. And I meant it," Mark said, his words calm and confident. Like he had absolutely no doubt that they would get the candles done.

"You've been so busy. When will you find time to help me?"

"I will make time. I think that's what we do anyway. We have time—everybody has the same amount. Some people just manage to get more accomplished in different things. Because they place their priorities in different areas. If we're getting married, my family will be my top priority, right after God. And that has to be the way it is."

She looked at him, so sincere, so upright, so confident in what he was saying. She believed him, believed he believed it, and meant what he said. She just didn't know too many people like that. They seemed to be tossed about with every wind, blown here and there, without too much effort on their part. But she felt like he was right. If they needed to make time for it, they could. It was a human thing.

"It doesn't help that my parents are arriving this evening too. I'm definitely nervous about that."

The boys were running around in the activity center, and they stood by the door, everything packed and ready to take over to her now-warm apartment, but he stood in front of her, grabbing her hands.

"Can we pray about that right now?" he asked softly.

Her eyes opened wide. She hadn't even considered praying about it. Of course, she spent a little bit of time in prayer every evening, but instead of being nervous, she should just give it to the Lord. She knew that.

She nodded. "Thank you for recommending it."

They bowed their heads, and he said a short prayer, asking God to alleviate her nervousness, to bless the time with family, and to strengthen and solidify the relationships between parent and child, grandparent and grandchildren. And Mark even said a little bit about himself, that God would grant him favor in her parents' eyes.

After he said amen, he didn't let go of her hand, but instead, when she opened her eyes, he was looking down at her with such love and tenderness that it was all she could do not to close the distance between them, wrap her arms around his neck, and press her lips to his.

"You're amazing," she said instead.

He shook his head, grinning and looking a little bashful. "All I did was pray."

"That wasn't all you did, but I appreciate it. Truly. Are you sure you want to be stuck with me for the rest of your life?" Sometimes she had this feeling of not being good enough for him. Or not that she wasn't good enough—that he deserved someone who was more spiritual, more considerate, less encumbered by the cares of this world, like her shop and her kids and the baggage with her parents.

"Absolutely. We haven't talked about a date, because I didn't want to pressure you."

"You suggested a Christmas wedding. I thought that sounded great."

"All right. Let me see what I can do to make that happen."

She nodded, but before she could say anything else, Aiden and

Ethan ran up, laughing and telling them about the funny thing that had just happened.

Mark dropped one of her hands, keeping hold of the other one, while he grabbed Ethan and picked him up.

Ethan had really opened up with Mark and was chatting away, talking more than Olivia had ever heard him speak.

That was just one more way that Mark had been good for her family.

Mark opened the door, and they walked across the parking lot, holding hands, heading over to unpack all of the things that Mark had just delivered to her apartment while she kept the boys.

Just before they got to her place, a car pulled up along the street. At first, Olivia couldn't figure out why it looked familiar, and then she recognized it.

"My parents! They're early!"

"They're probably really eager to see their long-lost daughter, and the grandchildren they've never met." Mark's words weren't censure, but they made a lot of sense.

"You're right. I guess I should've expected this."

She stood on the sidewalk while her parents got out of the car. Both of them looked almost exactly the same—maybe a few more wrinkles, a couple more gray hairs—but they still looked young, relatively speaking, and the smiles on their faces couldn't be bigger. If she had been nervous about the reaction to seeing her, she shouldn't have needed to worry. Her parents were not the kind of people to hold grudges. And maybe five years was more than enough time for all of them to have not spoken.

"Olivia!" her mother said, hurrying, pausing for a moment, as though unsure of Olivia's reaction, but when Olivia smiled and made a small move toward her, a huge grin broke out on her face, and she hurried toward Olivia with her arms out. "I've missed you so much!"

"I missed you too, Mom. More than I could ever say."

They hugged tight, and it felt good to be in her mother's arms again. She hadn't realized how much she had missed having a mom to depend on, someone to talk to, someone who loved her more than anything or anyone else in the world.

Her dad came over and hugged her too, and then she introduced them to the boys. She had been telling the boys that they were going to meet their grandparents, which didn't really mean a whole lot to them, but both of them seemed excited and interested as she introduced them. They weren't hard to tell apart, and her parents caught on right away.

"I haven't been in my apartment because the furnace quit working during the storm, and we were actually on our way over to unpack all the things that we've been using while we've been out." And that's when she realized she hadn't introduced Mark. "But I'm sorry. This is Mark—Pastor Mark." She paused for just a moment, not because she was embarrassed, but because it was unfamiliar. "My fiancé."

Her parents' eyes grew big, and they looked at her, then Mark, then each other.

"This is certainly different from the last time," her mom finally said. And then her mom shook her head and turned a beaming smile on Mark. "Pastor Mark. It's so nice to meet you. We're excited to welcome you into the family."

"We are. Whoever Olivia chooses will be treated like family by us."

Olivia's mouth wanted to drop open, but she kept it closed. It was obvious that her parents had done some soul-searching after the way they'd treated Cam.

They were right—she'd have to tell them that later. She shouldn't have married him. He wasn't a good Christian, and their marriage might not have lasted. But her parents hadn't been kind to him either. She supposed they'd both learned some lessons from that, and all of them were probably better people because of it.

"Thank you," Mark said. "I lost my parents a few years ago, and I'm excited to be getting new ones. God provides."

"He sure does," her mom agreed. Then her mom slipped her arm through Olivia's and said, "I sure hope you're going to be busy for the next week, because I can't wait to spend all day every day babysitting my grandchildren."

Olivia thought about how Mark had just said, "God provides." Boy, did He ever.

"You can't even begin to believe how busy I am, how many candle orders I have to fulfill, and how much I will appreciate you watching the children."

"I always love the way God works," her mom said.

Boy, Olivia did too. Her eyes met Mark's, and she knew they were both thinking the same thing. That God had worked everything out perfectly, even when it looked like He wasn't going to. With the storm, and all the orders, and her having no idea how they were going to be completed, and then they couldn't even get in because of the furnace being broken, and her getting backed up, and then her parents came, and it was like God rolled the clouds away, and she could see clearly that He had a plan all along.

It was a beautiful sight.

Chapter Twenty-Nine

Mark put the last bow on the last candle and stepped back. His back hurt, his shoulders ached, and his feet were almost numb, but they'd gotten all the candles done.

"Wow. I didn't know for sure whether we would get that finished or not," Olivia said, standing beside him, her arm around his waist.

He wrapped his arm around her shoulder and pulled her close to him.

"I knew we were gonna get it done," he said softly. Confident the way a man could be when he depended on God.

It was crazy the way God had worked in his life over the last couple of years, bringing him to Mistletoe Meadows, handing him the Secret Saint ministry, a church full of wonderful people who wanted to grow closer to God—and the numbers as well—and now, best of all, a wife and family of his own.

"We don't have too much time to admire it. You need to be at the church in forty-five minutes."

"I have some men coming to carry these boxes over for the candlelight service, so you don't need to worry about anything. And you need to be at the church in forty-five minutes too. I'm betting it takes you slightly longer to get ready than it does me."

She laughed. "If I had the boys, I'd agree with you, but I've barely seen them since my parents arrived. They've not wanted to let the boys out of their sight, and... it feels so good to have the family together."

"Yeah. Who would've thought that they would be here for our wedding?" They had decided that they would get married on Christmas Eve after the candlelight service, rather than on Christmas Day. Pastor Powell, retired from a church in the next town, was going to be officiating, and Mark, while he was very nervous—just because this was a huge step and he knew it—was looking forward to it. They'd already decided that the family would live at the parsonage, and Olivia had been talking about giving up her candle business so that she could be a full-time wife and mother and pastor's wife.

He wanted her to do what she felt God was leading her to, but he couldn't fault her for wanting to let the business go. He would prefer that she devote herself to the higher calling of being a mother and a wife and serving God through the church.

Although, he couldn't deny that the money would be nice.

However, he was one hundred percent confident that God would provide.

"I guess we'll have a story to tell our grandchildren, that we had forty-five minutes to prepare for our wedding."

He laughed. "I bet there are not too many people who got ready for their wedding in less time."

"I would imagine that you're right."

He hugged her, leaning down and pressing his lips to her forehead. He loved this woman with his whole heart and soul, and knew that he would spend the rest of his life doing everything in his power to be the best husband and father that he could possibly be. He was looking forward to it. He had spent enough time alone that he would appreciate every second of having someone beside him.

"All right. I'm gonna grab a box and carry it with me, and I'll be back over to walk you guys over to the church."

"All right. I'll make sure everyone's ready."

The candles were perfect for the candlelight service, and if Mark had to say so himself, it was possibly the nicest service he'd ever been in. Beautiful, spirit-filled, and with a reminder of Jesus and the gospel—that he came to earth not just to be born in a stable for us to celebrate Christmas, but because everything pointed to the cross. The suffering and the death and what Jesus gave up and sacrificed in order for mankind to be able to experience salvation. It was because of the great love of God, but salvation would not be possible without the suffering of Christ. No one really wanted to talk about suffering because everyone wanted to focus on happy things, but it was good to keep that in the forefront of one's mind, because one had a tendency to be more appreciative of the free gift of salvation when one remembered the cost that Jesus paid for it.

Still, as he stood beside Olivia, holding their candles and singing "Silent Night" with the rest of the congregation, he thought about his marriage ahead, and hopefully the decades that they would have together—the many, many Christmas services that they would share. He looked at Pastor Powell, his arm also around his wife, who did not look like she was doing very well. Pastor Powell hadn't said, and unfortunately, Mark realized he'd been too busy to ask. Perhaps this would be her last Christmas. Someday, forty years from now, he and Olivia would be standing in that same place. It could be sad, except they would be closer to heaven than they were right now, and that was the ultimate end—being with Jesus for eternity. This world was just a temporary place, no matter how cozy and wonderful it was.

But a temporary place that they had to do their best to live for the Lord in, until God decided to take them home.

Most of the folks who were at the Christmas Eve service in the packed church stayed for the wedding, since the church remained very crowded.

It was simple and beautiful, and Olivia was radiant as a bride.

Her parents stood in the front row with the boys between them, beaming as they watched their daughter get married. Mark had been so happy to see their relationship mended over the week that they'd spent getting to know each other again.

He knew that life wouldn't be perfect, but he also knew that Olivia appreciated her parents and their perspective much more than she did a few years ago.

"I now pronounce you man and wife. You may kiss your bride," Pastor Powell said, his eyes twinkling, as though he knew that this was the part that Mark had been looking forward to.

He bent down, kissing his wife, and appreciating the fact that this was just the first of many.

It wasn't a long kiss, but it was full of promise, as they broke apart and he looked into her eyes for just a moment. Yeah, there was a lifetime there. A lifetime of Christmases, of joy, of cozy evenings by the fire, of frantic days of work, of helping people in their community, of long days just doing the right thing.

All of that made a life, and he had to admit, he was looking forward to theirs.

A Gift from Jessie

View this code through your smart phone camera to be taken to a page where you can download a FREE ebook when you sign up to get updates from Jessie Gussman! Find out why people say, "Jessie's is the only newsletter I open and read" and "You make my day brighter. Love, love, love reading your newsletters. I don't know where you find time to write books. You are so busy living life. A true blessing." and "I know from now on that I can't be drinking my morning coffee while reading your newsletter – I laughed so hard I sprayed it out all over the table!"

Claim your free book from Jessie!

Escape to more faith-filled romance series by Jessie Gussman!

The Complete Sweet Water, North Dakota Reading Order:

Series One: Sweet Water Ranch Western Cowboy Romance (11 book series)

Series Two: Coming Home to North Dakota (12 book series)

Series Three: Flyboys of Sweet Briar Ranch in North Dakota (13 book series)

Series Four: Sweet View Ranch Western Cowboy Romance (10 book series)

Spinoffs and More! Additional Series You'll Love:

Jessie's First Series: Sweet Haven Farm (4 book series)

Small-Town Romance: The Baxter Boys (5 book series)

Bad-Boy Sweet Romance: Richmond Rebels Sweet Romance (3 book series)

Sweet Water Spinoff: Cowboy Crossing (9 book series)

Small Town Romantic Comedy: Good Grief, Idaho (5 book series)

True Stories from Jessie's Farm: Stories from Jessie Gussman's Newsletter (3 book series)

Reader-Favorite! Sweet Beach Romance: Blueberry Beach (8 book series)

Blueberry Beach Spinoff: Strawberry Sands (10 book series)

From Strawberry Sands to: Raspberry Ridge (12 book series)

Swoonfully Jolly Holiday Stories:

Holiday Romance: Cowboy Mountain Christmas (6 book series)

Cowboy Mountain Christmas Spinoff: A Heartland Cowboy Christmas (9 book series)

New and Much Loved: Mistletoe Meadows (4 books and counting!)

Laughing Through the Snow: Christmas Tree, PA Sweet Romcoms (6 short reads)